CENTERVILLE

An Historical Novel

by

Richard Otto Wiegand

ISBN: 978-1-7322171-7-1

TABLE OF CONTENTS

PART ONE

PART TWO

PART ONE

CHAPTER 1 – ARRIVAL

I arrived by ship in the small port village of Centerville in Manitowoc County, Wisconsin on a Monday in mid-1858. My journey south along the west shore of Lake Michigan from Green Bay and Algoma was uneventful. Not that I expected anything else, but the Great Lakes have had their share of shipwrecks. Lake Michigan can produce waves of 20 feet that can sink even the sturdiest ships. There were two small shipwrecks off Centerville shores that I became aware of from my research in modern times.

Not all shipwrecks can be blamed on the weather. One of the deadliest in Great Lakes history occurred on Lake Michigan in 1847 off Haven between the village of Centerville and the city of Sheboygan to the south. The *Phoenix*, a ship loaded with mostly Dutch immigrants, caught fire five miles offshore. About 250 people perished. Only 40 were saved. I remember being told this story from when I was growing up as a kid in Centerville township.

My captain, a middle-aged, French-Canadian with a handlebar mustache, made a scheduled stop in Manitowoc to pick up passengers headed to Milwaukee. "Are you sure you want to get off at Centerville?" he asked in English with his heavy French accent. "You'll have a better chance for a job on my next stop in Sheboygan. I wouldn't charge you any extra either. I hear that the shipping line may end regular passenger service to stops like Centerville. The place has been settled."

"Thanks, but I'm on a mission," I replied. "I'll take my chances with Centerville."

"I last stopped there about a year ago," the captain continued. "I think they changed the name of the village, but it is still listed as Centerville on my ship's log."

The village of Centerville got its name because it was located halfway between Manitowoc and Sheboygan. It also happened to be about halfway between Green Bay and Milwaukee. When the village tried to get a post office, it was turned down because a Centerville with a post office already existed in western Wisconsin. Having two post offices named "Centerville" in one state would have caused confusion with the mail. In the end, the village had to come up with a different name.

Legend has it that a local judge ended up being responsible for a new name. He used to hike the dozen or so miles from Manitowoc to Centerville on weekends, calling the place "Hika." The township remained Centerville, however, and most people at the time just continued to call the village Centerville. For myself, I preferred to refer to the village as Hika or just the village, and to the greater township as Centerville.

I pondered briefly about the location of Centerville next to Lake Michigan. Living next to a large body of water alters one's geographic perspective. One has only half of the normal dry land to deal with. In the case of Centerville, there is no east, just water. As a result, there are fewer places and people to learn about as well as fewer options to relocate or do business within a reasonable travel distance.

Lake Michigan also moderates the climate. Spring comes later, fall lasts longer. Different crops can be grown just a half hour inland from the lake. Depending on wind direction, Centerville residents can be cooler in the summer and warmer in the winter. East winds tend to be humid and raw. There can be considerable lake-effect snow, making winters difficult to navigate.

My journey on the ship provided me some solitude to think about what I might expect to see when I arrived. What were Hika and Centerville really like in the late 1850s? How many people and landmarks would I immediately recognize from my historical research?

My primary mission was to visit my ancestors who had settled in the area a century before I was born. What kind of people were they? I was so anxious to meet them. I had no idea what they even looked like. I had a ton of questions about them, the farm and the community. I was curious about their immigrant experience, the real reasons why they came to America. The opportunity to go back in time to meet them was incredibly daunting!

At the same time, the chance of getting caught up in the lives of my relatives and somehow altering the future was also a real fear for me. I understood that I did have some discretion for my mission, yet there were a lot of boundaries. There were things I couldn't do, say or become in the past. I guessed that I would just have to find out as I went along.

More than once was I tempted to turn around and immediately go back to the future. I was getting very nervous! I paced the deck. The captain looked at me and smiled but didn't say anything. He was used to seeing anxious people arriving for the first time from places afar. He couldn't have realized just how far I was coming from!

Hika had two piers. One was privately-owned and one was run by a farmer cooperative. Either could be used for loading or unloading large items. One of the piers was specifically designed with a broad end to turn a team of horses and wagon around on it.

Cordwood, shingles, lumber, hides and barrels were the main exports of the area, usually headed south to Milwaukee and Chicago. Imports were many and included tools, nails, iron, cloth, crock pots, canning jars, sugar, salt and coffee. Despite what the captain had thought about future passenger service to Hika, I knew that the piers would be needed for both passengers and cargo well into the 20th century.

After saying goodbye to the captain, I walked off the passenger pier with my two suitcases tracking uphill into the center of Hika, a mix of log and timber frame buildings. There were a few people around with horses and wagons, running errands, hauling much-needed supplies from the village to the countryside. Since the weather was good and it was a Monday, I expected that farmers were mostly busy at home.

Deciding to find a place to stay for a few nights before I went to my ancestor's farm, I stopped to ask the nearest person, a rough-looking woman of mixed descent, likely part Indian. She was startled, like someone who never expected to be asked for advice, much less talked to by a stranger.

"You can get a room at the New Settlement Tavern," the woman replied.

"Of course, the famous New Settlement Tavern!" I suddenly realized. It would become the longest continuously licensed tavern in the state, or so they claimed.

After giving me a questioning stare, she asked, "Where did you learn that German?" and then just as quickly hurried off.

"Stay away from that woman," a man said to me as he came up. "She has a bad reputation."

"Well, it takes two to tango, you know," I responded without thinking about where and when I was.

"What did you say?" the man asked, looking perplexed. Before I had time to explain myself, the man interjected. "What are you looking for?"

"A place to stay for a few nights," I replied.

"The New Settlement Tavern has some rooms upstairs above the bar, too noisy in my opinion," he said. "But it's cheaper."

"Or you can try the inn across the street, right there," as he pointed toward it. "It's a lot quieter."

"Do you know anyone around here?" he then asked, seeming to question my strange clothes and sudden appearance.

"I do," I said. "I'm a distant relative, but they are not expecting me. The Wagner family. The husband is not Saxon."

"Oh, you mean Alfred Wagner, the Lipper," he replied, nodding his head. "They live three miles straight west," he said, pointing in that direction.

"I know where the farm is," I caught myself before saying it aloud.

"They might put you to work. They are hard workers," the man continued. "Are you looking to settle and work?"

"For a while."

"The Wagners don't have much room. Small house, several children plus a hired man and a maid. You might have to sleep in the barn!" he laughed. "I guess it doesn't matter," he continued. "The house and the barn are the same building!"

"Why don't you just walk there today?" he said thoughtfully. "Or I could give you a ride for a few pennies."

"I prefer to wait," I said.

"By the way, what is your name?" he asked, taking a new interest in me.

"Otto Hamman" I replied, using the fictional name I decided to use for my mission. I was a direct Wagner descendent in real life, of course, but felt that I needed to use an alias as to not create any suspicion regarding my real identity.

"You are a Lipper too?" he asked.

"Yes."

"You should have brought a couple of your famous horses along from Europe," he joked. "Don't you call them Lipperzaners?"

"Lipizzaners!" I corrected him. "The horses are actually from Slovenia."

"Where did you learn that German?" he asked and walked away.

"I guess I'll have to work on my German," I thought to myself as I walked toward the tavern.

CHAPTER 2 – HIKA

I took a room at the New Settlement Tavern for a few days because I needed more time to gather up the courage to visit my ancestors. I also needed to get some supplies.

The tavern was every bit as rustic but less classy than its successor over a century later. Of course, the old photos of the village on the tavern wall that I was used to looking at during my previous visits were not there yet! The camera had barely been invented when I arrived in Centerville in 1858. Too bad I couldn't bring my modern, digital camera with me on this mission!

There was a dam on Centerville Creek behind the tavern with a water wheel that powered a sawmill. The constant noise of the sawmill annoyed me, but such was the price of progress. At least it didn't run at night. A flour and grist mill on the other side also ran on waterpower from the dam. The dam would wash out twice due to flooding in its early years. Later a flood would also take out one of the mills.

In 1858, Hika had a general store, butcher shop, doctor, barber, dentist, brewery, tannery, lumberyard, sawmill, cooper, shoe repair, two blacksmiths, two taverns and two churches. There was one business dedicated entirely to the timber cutting industry, no surprise of course, where one could purchase axes, wood malls, sledgehammers, hand saws, circle saws, cant hooks, various implement handles, splitting wedges, chains, files and stones for sharpening, stump pullers, and other implements and services related to tree destruction.

There was also a brickyard on the south side of the village. The unusual yellow clay found there was used for making what were called "cream city" bricks. Three Wagner buildings would be constructed in the later part of the 1800s using these bricks. A century later cream city bricks were so popular and rare that they would often be recycled into newer decorative construction.

The doctor in Hika had a room for seeing patients at his residence, but he preferred to make house calls instead. All the devices and medications that he needed to check and treat his patients would fit in his black bag or in his buggy. There were no hospitals in this part of the state at the time. The general thought was that if you were going to get well, you would get well better at home. If you were going to die, you would die better at home.

The Lutheran church and Catholic church were located within a block of each other. They shared a cemetery, split by a fence.

Marriages between the two faiths were frowned on by both sides. Many immigrants who settled in Centerville still had memories of religious wars in Europe and weren't keen on giving up the acrimony. To listen to some of the vitriol coming from pulpits even in my time in the future, converting to the other side was a veritable fast track to hell! Some things never change.

When there was the threat of a "mixed" marriage, considerable pressure from both sides was exerted to either convert or back out of the marriage. Lutherans were especially hostile to the Catholic Church which insisted that children from marriages with Catholics be brought up as Catholics. If the Catholic parent didn't agree, he or she could be excommunicated. The Catholics continue this demand to the present day, although the pressure to comply has been greatly reduced and the retribution largely eliminated. The Lutherans for a long time regarded the Catholic Church as a "bully institution."

There was a couple in the village, however, who defied the marriage norm. People joked that they would someday be buried next to each other, one on the Lutheran side of the cemetery fence and one on the Catholic side. That was indeed what happened! Years later, the fence was removed when the churches were gone. The cemeteries were combined, although still maintained under separate funding. The couple was no longer separated in death by religion or fence. Love triumphed over physical and religious boundaries!

It had rained the day before I arrived. The village streets were muddy, and it was hard to find a dry surface to walk on. There were cobble stones on only a few surfaces in the village.

"Why don't you put down some gravel?" I asked someone later at the tavern.

"What is that?" the man replied. "Oh, you mean those small stones found in pits! We don't have much of that around here."

I could have told the locals where there was plenty of gravel nearby but decided to drop the subject. I knew that one farmer just north of the village would almost go broke trying to farm his gravelly soil, while the next owner would make a ton of money mining the gravel. "No matter where you live, there is always a gold mine beneath your feet," my dad had told me, repeating the oft-mentioned axiom. "You just need to figure out what that gold is."

The future gravel pit was located about a mile from a small bridge where the body of the first white man murdered in the county was discovered earlier in the decade. There was a love triangle. A man and his friend murdered another man over a dispute about a girlfriend. The body was hidden under the bridge. The perpetrators fled to the western part of the state, leaving the girlfriend behind. One of the men briefly returned to visit Centerville a few decades years later. He was not apprehended.

Chapter 3 – Family

The second day I started asking around about my Wagner relatives. "You might see them in the village on Saturday," I was told by a young man who seemed to know who everyone was. "Alfred Wagner is the Justice of The Peace for the township. He sometimes has business at the township office which is located here in the village."

Someone asked me if I knew about Alfred's background.

Lying, I said, "I didn't."

"Well he supposedly shot and killed someone back in Europe, forcing him to flee. I don't know how he got to be Justice of The Peace, but I suppose he knows how to handle a gun! He's not Saxon, you know. We can barely understand his dialect around here. Thankfully we use High German to communicate. Alfred does speak pretty good English."

Centerville was a mix of Germans of various origins, not just Saxon, but from kingdoms as diverse and far apart as Baden, Bavaria, Schleswig, Mecklenburg and Prussia. Each group often formed its own small community around a small church or school. The Wagner neighborhood, I knew, was largely Saxon.

"What about Wagner's wife?" I asked.

"Christina came over before he did. They met here. I heard that her father in Saxony was sleeping with the maid and divorced her mother. Christina came with her first husband, Friedrich Meyer, and a brother Gustav Freiburg and his wife Natalie. The Freiburgs live next door to Christina. Meyer died soon after they came, as well as the baby, from scarlet fever, I heard. Wagner just drifted in one day looking for work and ended up marrying her."

"The Wagner children?" I questioned.

"Three small ones. Another died. There is a young woman too, a Meyer cousin. Pretty but different. Elsa Lorraine Jacoby is her name, the man said rather assuredly. I remember her middle name because Lorraine is also my mother's name," he continued. "Elsa works as the maid. I like her. I tried dating her, but it didn't work out. The moment you think you got Elsa on your arm, you don't."

"Elsa has some baggage too," the man continued. "She had a falling out with her family in Sheboygan County, so she moved in with the Wagners. There are rumors about her family that I won't say. You may find something out. Her brother also moved out. He killed himself last year. He was just 20 years old. He helped at the Wagners sometimes."

"Why did he kill himself?" I asked too quickly.

"Some problem with the father is all I heard. Hung himself in a tree just north of the Wagner homestead," the man replied. "I think it was on the neighbor's side of the fence where he was helping to build a shed. Elsa found him. She is still having a hard time with all of that. I tried to console her."

"Thanks for telling me so I don't bring it up when I go to the farm." I replied.

"The Wagner homestead is right next to the property line," he added. "Usually settlers try to locate their buildings more in the center of their property along the road, but the Wagners have a side hill and a low spot in the middle. You'll see why they built where they did when you go there."

"How do you know them again?" the man asked.

"I'm related to the Wagners back in the old country."

"Well, don't ask me any more questions," he said. "Go see them for yourself. I'm sure you have plenty of catching up to do."

"I'm sure I do," I replied.

"Welcome to Centerville!" the man said smiling.

Chapter 4 – Gennie

I spent my few days in the village planning my visit to the Wagner farm while still hoping to get more information on the Wagners. In the meantime, I was getting to know some people in the village.

The so-called woman of ill-repute, Gennie Sunshine, would sometimes eat or drink at the tavern. People said that she drank whiskey, smoked, gambled and swore, behaviors not acceptable for a woman of the time, but I didn't see her do any of those when I was around. I rather enjoyed her chatter. Gennie complained about a lot of things, often in English, usually bucking the established thought of the day.

"Why don't women have the right to vote?" she complained one day.

I would find out that Gennie once had a husband, but they divorced. They had two children. Then she had two more children while not married. Having children without a proper husband seemed to be Gennie's problem in the community, not the false claims of prostitution by some. I got the impression that Gennie was struggling to make the best of a less-than-desirable situation.

Gennie was sensitive about her ancestry. "The Indians wouldn't hurt anyone!" she shouted once in the tavern. "It's the white people that do all the damage!"

The few Indians left in the county, mostly north of Manitowoc, were suffering from alcoholism and diseases brought by the white man. I wanted to tell Gennie that she was exactly right. There would be no Indians left in the county in a couple of decades.

The original tribe in the region were the Menominee with their various bands. Centerville was part of territory ceded by the tribe to the government in the 1830s. Other than Gennie, I saw little evidence of the people who once occupied the area. "It was a shame," I thought. The original residents, minding their own business, were suddenly attacked, killed or forced out and then almost completely forgotten. I often wondered while growing up on the farm what Indian ghosts might be still be lurking there.

Gennie also complained about slavery in the South. She asked another tavern patron if he thought there was going to be a war over slavery.

"You can bet on that!" I said too quickly but didn't want to say anymore. The war would start in another couple of years. There was a lot of tension between the North and the South that one could sense just from conversation, even if you didn't read the newspapers.

I met an older fellow at the tavern named Hubert Schmidt. Schmidt was a Protestant name in Hika while Schmitt was the Catholic version. People said Hubert was seen at the tavern almost every day, usually around noon, always drinking hard liquor. He was from Mecklenburg, a northern German state. Hubert worked in the brickyard, tending the kilns early in the morning and then again in the afternoon.

"How does Hubert get away with drinking so much?" I asked Gennie.

"He works it off," she said. "He otherwise eats well and stays trim.

He lives in the next township, riding his horse in every day. His minister and his doctor both told him to stop drinking if he wanted to get old. Both the minister and doctor died at relatively young ages," she said. "Hubert is in his early 70s and still working hard." I knew that he would later give up work and drinking and live to be almost 90.

CHAPTER 5 – SHEEPSHEAD

I walked around the village. Although a few immigrants were probably still arriving, I figured that the villagers would know almost everyone else who lived here. Although the village was growing to be sure, the population of the township was quite large, given the small sizes of the many farms and the large sizes of the families on them.

Several people looked at me curiously as if they knew I was a newcomer. I also realized that they may have been looking at my strange clothes.

The third day I visited the general store, hoping to find more appropriate and comfortable clothes. Before I came on this mission, I had managed to find what I thought were period-appropriate clothes at a vintage costume store. I never liked suspenders and found that I really didn't like buttons where the zipper was supposed to be. Of course, zippers had not yet been invented. My shoes were terribly uncomfortable. The dead guy who once wore them must have been hastened to the grave by sore feet! "I'll find new clothes and get shoes made just for me," I mumbled to myself as I entered the store.

Inside the general store, I saw men playing a card game on top of a barrel. A popular pastime for German settlers was a card game called "sheepshead." (German *"schafkopf,"* or "barrel head".) Men often played it, just like I observed here, on the top of a barrel in a general store. Men and sometimes women played it at family parties.

Sheepshead is played with 32 cards. Diamonds are often trump as well as all queens and jacks. Non-trump cards are called fail. Queens are high followed by jacks. The most powerful queens and jacks are clubs, spades, hearts and diamonds in that order.

The game is usually played with four players, but one can play alone, with another person, or even up to seven or eight persons with two decks. Some people gambled, playing for pennies, but it was often just a contest of points. Pennies in my time weren't worth much, but in the 1850s could buy a small tool or a beer.

There are other unusual characteristics of the game including the point system that I won't elaborate on here. Sheepshead is probably the most unconventional card game I ever played.

I grew up with the game. Sheepshead was notably played in Wisconsin from the Illinois border to Green Bay and about 50 miles inland from Lake Michigan. If you were born in that part of the state in the 1900s and didn't play sheepshead, there was something wrong with you!

Some of the Centerville sheepshead rules in the 1850s were a bit different, but I knew I could get back into the game quite easily if I wanted to.

I asked the players in the store if they had ever played for the least points, a version called "leasters." Leasters were a nice change of pace, resulting in more laughs and shouting than the usual version. The men replied that they had.

"Do you require the winner with the least points to at least take one trick with one or more points?" I asked.

"We do," was the reply. I told the players I would join them one day for a friendly round or two.

CHAPTER 6 – TOWNSHIP

I stayed in the village for four days, deciding to hold my room at the tavern for at least another week. Since I was pretending to be a distant relative of the Wagners for the mission, but in reality was a total stranger, I didn't want the Wagners to feel obligated to put me up. I had no idea what kind of reception I would get. At best, I would hopefully spend a few months meeting and learning about the Wagners. At worst, my visit to the past would be much shorter.

On Friday morning it was time to walk to the Wagner farm. I was impressed to see acres of dense, native forest, just west of the village. When later parceled and isolated, these patches of forest would be called "woods or woodlands" by the locals.

I was not surprised but still shocked by the extent of the clearing that was going on. Centerville settlers had wrecked considerable damage on the forest. The entire township, originally covered with forest, was parceled and settled in just ten years.

The cleared land that I observed along the road exposed patches of virgin soil so black and rich that it was hard for me to believe. The rich topsoil would allow farmers to grow bountiful crops without much additional fertility for three generations. Almost all the virgin forest would unfortunately be cleared by the end of the century. Most of that beautiful topsoil would be lost to erosion in the next hundred years.

There were so many birds! I paused for several minutes trying to identify them.

My focus turned to the large flocks of pigeons. It took a few moments before I realized what I was seeing. These were passenger pigeons! One of my ancestors in Sheboygan County said that the flocks were so large when settlers first came there that when the birds took to the air, they blocked out the sun!

I sensed both profound awe and shame. I got down on my knees in respect. The millions of passenger pigeons that existed in the 1850s would all be gone in less than 60 years, becoming extinct in 1914. I then thought about the millions of bison on the Great Plains that would nearly go extinct in the next 30 years. "What hath man wrought!" I thought, trying to mimic the Bible.

The future Village of Cleveland, just west of Hika, was of course not there yet. It was just another farm, still mostly trees. In addition to the ship captain, people in the village told me that there were plans for a railroad. I knew that the railroad would come through in 1873 just west of Hika. The new village that grew up along the railroad would eventually overwhelm and incorporate Hika as well as another small village to the west called St. Wendel. By 1858, there was another Catholic church in St. Wendel. It would later take in the parishioners from Hika when its Catholic church closed in the 1950s.

The second mile on my way to the Wagners featured a farm on the north, owned by a Klemme who would marry into my greater family. The first generations of Klemmes would be better at masonry and construction than farming. Focusing strongly on education, the family would later produce teachers, clergymen and a legislative historian, the first person with a Master of Arts degree from Centerville.

Land in the Centerville area was purchased from owner-speculators, some of whom were given tracts in exchange for military service. This practice was common after the War of 1812. The going price for un-cleared land in Centerville in 1848 was $1.25 per acre. The first land purchases had to be registered with the land office located in Green Bay, fifty miles to the north. Some early settlers, not yet having horses, had to walk the entire distance to register their land.

Any Indians who once lived in the area were now gone, losing bat-tles with whites and their diseases, and being forced to live on reser-vations. Evidence of their earlier presence consisted mainly of arrow heads, stone axe heads and burial mounds. All of these would be found in Centerville. The burial grounds discovered two miles northeast of the Wagner farm would be looted to gain a dime or two. A 10,000-year-old former Indian village would be discovered in northwestern Sheboygan County.

CHAPTER 7 – NEIGHBORHOOD

The third mile, now almost to my destination, featured the Hessel family on the north and the Kaiser family on the south. The Hessels came from Europe with the Meyers and Freiburgs in 1848. From New York, the three families came via the Erie Canal and the Great Lakes, arriving in Centerville in late July three weeks later. The families quickly built a large log house on the Hessel farm, staying together there until the Meyers and Freiburgs could build their own houses. The Kaisers settled two years later.

Most of the immigrant farmers in the immediate area where the Wagners lived came from Saxony. The north-south road that I was approaching, a military road later called Union Road, would be known locally as Saxon Road. The grade school just to the north on that road would be called Saxon School. The cemetery in the same direction, originally called God's Little Acre, would become Saxon Cemetery. The Lutheran church located next to the cemetery would however, sticking with tradition, be named after an apostle.

The Kaisers were indeed from Saxony and were indeed proud

Germans. However, descendants found out later that their family surname was not German. The Kaisers were part of a Slavic group called "Sorbian" or "Wende" that was absorbed into Saxony.

We would find out over time through genealogy research and DNA testing that none of us were as German as we thought we were. Although the ancestors may have all come from German states or kingdoms, considerable mixing occurred previously in Europe, sometimes only a few generations before. Over the centuries, European boundaries were changing all the time. Ethnic groups might be shuffled across the landscape.

My DNA revealed small portions of genetics from several other nationalities including British, Dutch, Polish, Russian, Ukrainian, Greek and Jewish. In the end, I could perhaps be content to be just half German, whatever that meant!

The original Kaisers settled in Ozaukee County in 1848, establishing a house and inn called the Leipzig House. Two of the sons purchased farms in Town Centerville in 1850. Arriving late in the year, they chose not to immediately build a house but to begin clearing the land. Commuting between the two locations, the Kaisers built a simple lean-to shelter in Centerville for the winter. They left one side of the shelter open to continuously pull trees into the fire on the house floor, saving on having to chop wood.

Several farms in the neighborhood would remain in the same families for over a hundred years. The Kaisers and Wagners have been neighbors for one-hundred and sixty years and counting.

CHAPTER 8 – FARM

The road I was on, later known as West Washington Avenue, ended at a T-intersection with Saxon Road. The Wagner farm was across on the left. I paused for several minutes to look at the buildings. "This was it, the same Wagner farm that I grew up on!" I said to myself. Although the farmstead looked small and primitive, I could hardly contain my excitement with what I saw!

There was a long, single-story, hewn-log building on the north side of the homestead that I realized was the Wagner housebarn. I was very curious to see this mysterious structure that was long gone by the time I was born. There was no mention of the housebarn in our oral history when I was growing up.

A small building to the west I guessed to be the well house. In later years, a milk house would be located over the well. I opened the old well at one point when I was farming to discover that it was about four feet across and 33 feet deep with bricks around the top and then stones down the sides. When I opened it, the water level was about four feet from the top. If the water table had been the same in 1848, why or how could they have dug down by hand to 33 feet? The water table must have changed, I thought. Perhaps it had something to do with the varying levels of Lake Michigan just three miles away. Or there were other sources of water or surface run-off related to the homestead that later contributed to the increase in the height of the water table. Among the many questions I had stored up in my mind for the Wagners, one would certainly be about the mysterious well.

A separate barn on the west side of the homestead, about 30 by 60 feet, appeared to be near completion. This would be the machine shed that I knew when I was growing up. I remember remnants of cow stanchions and horse stalls in it.

I then saw three other buildings that I knew nothing about from our farm history, one to the east of the housebarn, possibly a woodshed, one to the southeast, no doubt an outdoor toilet, and one to the south, possibly a chicken house.

Original farmsteads usually started in a clearing with a rustic temporary house, often made of logs, on the intended north side. In some cases, the house was combined with or attached to a barn as was common in Europe. Livestock would be located on the west end. Second-floor bedrooms may be located above the livestock to capture animal heat.

Everything was designed for the weather. Prevailing winds and winter cold would come from the north and west. The next building on the farmstead would be a barn to the west. When the time came to build a new frame or brick house, it would be located to the southeast using existing structures as windbreaks. Called a "courtyard system", the Wagner farmstead was developing exactly in this way.

Chapter 9 – Elsa

Still gathering my courage, I took a deep breath, then walked to the driveway and up a slight grade to the west toward the house. To the right of the house door was a small fenced enclosure containing the graves of Friedrich Meyer, the first husband of Christina Freiburg Wagner, and their infant son, Hans. The grave markers were metal crosses as I had been told. The crosses and the enclosure were removed long before my time, around 1912. The house door was open. No one was about, but I could hear children playing inside. There was not even a dog to welcome me.

I noticed a garden near the chicken barn. A young woman was working in it, hoeing weeds between rows of vegetables. As I approached the garden, the woman looked up in surprise.

"Hello! Who are you?" she asked.

This must be Elsa Jacoby, I realized. She was rather tall, dark-haired, slim and attractive, with an air of independence about her. Elsa had a weathered appearance that made her look older than her actual age that I guessed to be about 25 years. Her clothes did not help. Elsa wore expressive, colorful clothes, but that were worn and dirty. Her hair was messy, strands of it slipping out of the kerchief she was wearing to hold it up. I somehow expected her, as a proper woman of the time would do when meeting a stranger, especially a man, to apologize for her appearance, but that did not happen.

I knew almost nothing of Elsa from family lore. She was only tangentially connected to the family through the Meyers. Like hired men, maids came and went. From my research, however, I knew that she died in childbirth and the location of the cemetery where she was buried. One story about her did come down through family lore that I distinctly remembered. Elsa once had a man in her life who suddenly left her and broke her heart. I was curious to find out more about that story.

"I'm sorry to surprise you," I apologized in my modern German, still trying with some difficulty to speak more like the people I was meeting. "My name is Otto Hamann. I just arrived from Detmold in Lippe Kingdom. I believe I am a distant relative of Alfred Wagner. I found that out when I moved to Detmold from Furstensburg, a small town in Lippe. However, I don't know much about the family. For some reason, people wouldn't talk to me much about Alfred except to say that he had been a glassmaker."

I went on to tell Elsa a number of lies to support my fictitious background. I decided to move to America because my parents were both dead, my sister had married and moved away, and I didn't have enough close family or friends to hold me. I declined to join a relative's printing business. There also was a lot of political and economic turmoil in Lippe, as in much of Europe, so when I found out that Alfred was here, I decided to visit and perhaps settle nearby.

The Lippe kingdom, or "principality", located in northwest Germany, later became part of Westphalia. At the time it was called "Lippe-Detmold," with Detmold being the capital. The soils of the area were particularly good for making glassware and pottery. Town Herman in Sheboygan County was named after an ancient German war hero from that region who fought off the Romans. There was a statue of Herman in Detmold.

Elsa stood with her mouth open during my long introduction as if she had just met a ghost. "Of course, I am a ghost from the future," I thought to myself.

Finally, after taking in my strange form of speech and unique story, Elsa resumed her introduction. "I'm glad you came, I mean, welcome," she said nervously. "I'm Elsa Jacoby, a cousin of Christina's first husband, Friedrich Meyer, buried over there." She pointed toward the grave.

I almost said, "I already know that," but caught myself. I need to be careful here, I had to remind myself, to stick with my mission, my alias, my story and the pretension of ignorance about the Wagners and Centerville that came with it.

Again, Elsa stood for a moment, sizing me up, smiling. She seemed to like what she saw. "I heard there was a handsome stranger in the village," she said. "It must have been you. People are always trying to get me married off, even to men I haven't met, especially to men I haven't met!" she laughed. Then she looked away embarrassed.

I was beginning to like this woman, I thought to myself. She certainly doesn't hesitate to tell me what's on her mind. I've only been here four days and Elsa has already heard about me! Word sure gets around fast! And I've already been paired up with her! Well, I'd rather be paired up with Elsa than Gennie, I supposed.

"Alfred is not here right now," Elsa said. "Alfred and Hugo are at the Freiburgs, working on a building."

"Hugo?" I asked.

"Hugo Heimerl, the hired man," Elsa replied. "Who is this man?" I wondered.

"The last time a strange man showed up here, it was Alfred himself, looking for work," Elsa continued, staring inquisitively at me. "He got a wife and a farm in the deal! Maybe it's too early to ask what you are really here for!" Again, Elsa was letting her imagination travel faster than necessary.

"Are you hungry?" Elsa asked, quickly changing the subject. "We eat lunch in another two hours, but you can have coffee, bread and butter, or some cakes now." Elsa was acting the part of the gracious host, of course, but somehow trying too hard to please me.

"Do you eat lard on bread?" I asked rather humorously, knowing that my dad and his siblings used to take lard sandwiches to grade school for lunch. They give one a lot of energy in the wintertime, but never sounded too appealing.

"Only in the winter," Elsa replied, looking surprised at my odd request.

"How about some chocolate?" I again joked.

"If you want to pay for it!" she replied. "We only have chocolate at Christmas! You are hard to please!" she complained with a smile.

"Elsa, I'll take whatever you have!"

I wanted to change the conversation to something else when Elsa suddenly shouted toward the house, "Christina, we have company!"

Three children emerged from the house, first the oldest, a girl, about six, then two little boys. Christina came out carrying a baby. She was dressed in black and looked rather stern.

"Who is this young man?" she asked Elsa. I briefly introduced myself.

"Alfred never mentioned you," Christina stated. "He does tend to keep his secrets. Never mind, he will come home before dark." She then smiled a bit. "Welcome to our house! You met Elsa. These are my children."

"What are their names?" I asked, already knowing the names.

"Emma, Alfred Junior, Ludwig and Heinrich, the baby. Are you thirsty? We have coffee."

"Thanks, I can wait until lunch if that's okay with you," I replied.

I looked with special interest at little Ludwig, my future great-grandfather, who would be an outstanding farmer and community leader. Christina went back inside. The children continued to stare at me.

"Where are you staying?" Elsa asked.

"At the New Settlement Tavern."

"You shouldn't stay there," Elsa said. "That place is not nice."

"It seems just fine to me," I replied.

"Do you have money?"

"Some," I said.

"You are alone?"

"Yes."

"Do you want to work?"

"Eventually," I smiled.

"I was hoping that you were a nobleman or professor," Elsa ventured. "There are too many common folks around. Educated men are more my style!" As much as I wanted to impress Elsa on the spot, I could not tell her that I really was a professor.

"We don't have much room here," Elsa continued. "The Hessels have a big log house and are almost moved into their new frame house. The Freiburgs, who are Christina's brother and sister-in-law, along with the Meyers and Hessels, lived together in that log house the first year. They didn't have time to each build their own house before winter set in. The log house has plenty of room. I will ask if you can stay there until you get settled."

"Thank you," I replied graciously. I was anxious to see what a log house for three families would look like.

I was surprised that Elsa was so quickly proposing these arrangements for an absolute stranger and without asking Alfred or Christina. She seemed anxious to keep me around, I noticed with growing interest.

"We'll get it sorted out," I assured Elsa.

Elsa asked, or rather directed me, to help her in the garden with the weeding. I noticed that there were at least two-dozen different vegetables. Diets were more diverse in those days as compared to the late 20th century when we thought that French fries, chips, corn syrup, ketchup and other processed plant products were all we needed from the garden to round out our high-protein and high-fat diets. I would see no obese children during my stay in Centerville and few obese adults.

Later, Elsa had me fill the wood box in the house entrance.

"Do you know how to milk a cow?" she asked.

"I do," I replied, not relishing the thought of milking a cow by hand. Although I grew up on a dairy farm, machines did most of that work. Milking the Wagner cow, however, would likely be an easier task, yielding no more than ten pounds of milk per day, as compared to my 40 cows that gave forty pounds each.

When Christina came out of the house again, she told Elsa to stop making me work. "He's our guest! Get a couple of benches and relax for the rest of the morning!"

There were no outdoor chairs. "Those damned Germans have no time to relax!" I mumbled to myself, "and certainly not during the day!" I was happy that Elsa, who was herself mumbling something to Christina, did not seem to hear me.

If the Germans, being tired and over-worked much of the time, would have had lawn chairs with backs, they would have immediately dozed off! Even when I was growing up, the idea of sitting outside during the day, except on Sundays, was totally foreign. If we did that, people would accuse us of being lazy. The idea of relaxing when the sun was up was unacceptable behavior in my German upbringing.

Elsa and I grabbed two benches. She moved us away from the house door to a tree on the opposite side of the graves. It was obvious that she wanted more privacy for us to converse.

Elsa continued asking questions about me. I tried to remain vague, given my mission, but still sound convincing. I could tell that she was having trouble believing everything I said but wanted to believe me anyway. The fictitious story of my Lipper background was somewhat sketchy. I threw in a lie about having an English nanny, hence my dialect. Whichever way my lies and her doubts added to the intrigue, Elsa apparently enjoyed it.

"So, you speak English then?" Elsa blurted out in English herself.

Elsa told me she knew how to handle a rifle, something that no doubt added to her exotic reputation in the community as I was beginning to discover. She said she would often shoot rabbits and squirrels. "I shoot those damned pigeons too," she bragged.

"Please don't do that!" I said too forcefully, considering the dire future of the passenger pigeons.

"Why not?" she asked. "There are so many. They are small but taste good!" Elsa looked at me curiously, sensing she hit a nerve about the pigeons.

"I'll explain it sometime," I replied, trying to act normally.

Elsa assumed that I knew how to hunt. When I told her that I was not really interested in hunting, she was surprised.

"How would you survive in the wild?" she questioned? How would you feed yourself? How would you fight off Indians if they attacked?"

"It's okay to call them Indians, but they are more appropriately referred to as Native Americans or members of The First Nation," I interjected without considering what century I was now in. "They are not from India."

Elsa again looked taken aback at my lecturing. "I have never heard of those names," she replied. "But they call themselves Indians, don't they?"

I told Elsa that my family in Lippe was urban and didn't engage in hunting, even thought it was a common sport among the more elite of society. Several of the family were teachers and government employees.

I reminded her that Lippe had not long before been under control of Napoleon and that many died in his wars. "Lippers were tired of war and guns," I said. "Besides, I think the Indians are in no condition to attack us anymore."

Elsa then talked about Saxony. She clearly missed her childhood home and friends there. Some still wrote, but they were slowly fading into history. It had been ten years since she left. Most of her immediate family and close relatives had moved to Sheboygan County.

Other than letters, there was no realistic way to communicate with the old country. Given the many reasons immigrants had to leave Europe or the many obstacles preventing a return visit, people inevitably lost track of one another. Many people that I talked to were often sad about the past. The decision to leave the old country, relatives and friends was never easy given that most knew they would never see each other again. Families and generations were ripped apart.

People lost touch even in America. There was a story of two brothers who migrated to northeastern Wisconsin at different times. They lived less than fifty miles apart but died never knowing where the other had settled. It was the grandchildren who finally connected the families.

Elsa wouldn't tell me why she wasn't living with her family, or why her brother Arlen, never mentioned in our conversations, had committed suicide. In later years, Arlen was somehow associated with the Wagner farm, even though we had no evidence that he ever lived there. It was when I reached Centerville on this mission that some confirmed that Arlen occasionally worked at the Wagner farm.

During our conversations, I saw that Elsa would at one moment have a cheerful disposition and then suddenly turn sorrowful about something in her past. I hoped that I would eventually find out at least a little of what her story was. I discovered quickly that I wanted to hug and console her as if she were a close relative or best friend even though our acquaintance was but a couple of hours old. There was some positive chemistry between us that I couldn't explain but was certainly drawing us together. It was almost as if we had known each other before.

CHAPTER 10 – HOUSE

I only saw the kitchen and dining room on my first visit to the Wagner residence located in the east part housebarn. Elsa showed me around while Christina went out to fetch some water. The walls were white plaster. The windows were small with only four panes in a frame. The panes were made of the typical, wavy, blueish-looking glass of the time that let the light in but were somewhat hard to look through. There were only throw rugs on the wooden floor, no carpeting. The kitchen table and chairs were locally-made and not fancy. There were two easy chairs and a sofa. One sensed that this was never intended to be a permanent house.

The kitchen table was off to one side of the room. Instead of chairs along the wall, there was a long box built into the wall that served as a bench to sit on while eating at the table. Usually the children sat on it. The top of the bench was a hinged cover. These box-benches were used for storage, usually for something not needed very often. I remember one at a neighbor's house containing winter clothes. I sat on a few of these benches in my youth. They were common in German houses.

The pot-bellied stove, the only source of heat in the house, looked familiar. Then I realized it was probably the same stove that was in the summer kitchen on the farm when I was growing up. Even the stove pipes looked the same.

Those old stoves and pipes were notorious for soot buildups and chimney fires. I asked if the Wagners ever had any chimney fires.

"Yes," Elsa said. "We've had some here. We lower a log chain down the chimney several times a year to clean it out. We then pull the pipes to clean them. The firewood needs to be good and dry, of course, to help to avoid a soot buildup."

I asked Elsa if the Wagners still had their immigrant trunk. "Sure, it's in the main bedroom," she said. "The room is kind of messy. We'll show it to you another time. You didn't bring a trunk?"

"No," I replied. "Two suitcases were all I needed."

Immigrant trunks were special. Each family had one, sometimes two. They were huge, often about four feet long by two-and-a-half or three feet wide and close to three feet high. They had two large handles, one on each end, a slightly-rounded cover and a large latch with a padlock. Trunks were made of wood with metal reinforcements on the outside, especially on the corners. Sometimes there would be decorations. Apart from suitcases and satchels or purses, the rest of the family's entire worldly possessions would have to fit in the trunk for the trip to America including clothes, bedding, cookery, and perhaps the Bible, jewelry or other important items like a broad axe and froe.

I excused myself to use the Wagner outdoor toilet or outhouse. There was a raised sitting area with two holes and covers. When one side was full, there was still a second side. Some had smaller holes for children.

When the excrement got too high, it was removed with a shovel from behind the building via a hinged, horizontal door. It was the same design as our outhouse on the farm when I was growing up.

In some parts of the world, a deep hole would be dug under the toilet, called a "long drop." When it filled up, it would be closed, and the building relocated to a new deep hole.

The Wagner outhouse in the 1850s had no toilet paper, just a bucket of water with a brush and a couple of towels hanging on the wall. No proverbial corn cobs here. The Wagners were not yet planting corn at that time.

CHAPTER 11 – CHRISTINA

After lunch, Christina and I talked for a while. Elsa had gone back to the garden. Christina seemed like a sad woman. I got the impression that she sometimes regretted having left Saxony. America had not been kind to her. She lost her first husband Friedrich Meyer and son shortly after arrival. She lost her first infant with Wagner, a daughter named Emily.

We never found the grave of little Emily in my time, but assumed she was buried in a local cemetery. The only evidence I found of Emily was on the 1850 Census, recorded in June of that year. She was listed as four months of age. Emily was never mentioned anywhere else, not in family lore, not on any existing cemetery stone, not even in any church record. An article in a Manitowoc County history in 1912 about the early history of the Wagners did not count her in the number of children born.

Elsa told me later that Emily was buried in a small cemetery near the Evangelical church on Union Road. I would go one day to visit the grave to see where it was. A small marker on the gravesite was no longer there in my time.

The trip to Centerville was not easy for the Freiburgs, Hessels and Meyers. The Atlantic journey was rough, with high waves and illness aboard the ship. Several passengers were ill, including the Meyers. When they finally reached New York after ten weeks at sea, there was talk of sending the entire shipload of passengers back. The captain, facing quarantine, downtime and potential refunds, dismissed the seriousness of the situation, blaming it on rough seas. He persuaded the authorities to let him disembark his passengers and head back to Europe. No person was quarantined.

Christina's husband Friedrich was still ailing when he got off the ship. He did his best to hide it. In addition to illness, Christina was also pregnant. The family made the three-week trip from New York to Centerville without incident. They appeared to recover. The Freiburgs and Hessels were not seriously affected by illness.

Not long after arrival, Christina gave birth. Then after two months, Friedrich and his infant son Hans suddenly succumbed to scarlet fever, according to a granddaughter I interviewed a century later. Christina survived.

Scarlett fever is not necessarily fatal. My father got it when he was young and recovered from it. There was some question in my mind that Friedrich and Hans may have died from another disease. I planned to find out more from Elsa.

Another granddaughter of Christina, nearing death in her mid-nineties, claimed in an interview with me that Christina's brother Gustav stole some of her money on the ship while she and Friedrich were fighting off their illnesses. I have never been able to substantiate this. Christina and her brother lived peacefully on neighboring farms. Descendants were always friendly. No rumors of grudges. The same granddaughter also claimed that Christina and her brother were illegitimate children, a story refuted by my research in Germany.

My impression in dealing with the oral history of my family after only a century and a half in America, especially after my research on Christina, was that not only was a portion of the story lost, but it had also changed over time. Perhaps no more than half of what remained of Christina's story turned out to be true.

Christina's story increased my concern about depending too much on oral history as a single source. I understand that oral history may be the only historical evidence that we have. A considerable portion of religious belief in the world is based on oral history that was only written down centuries later. It is important to back up oral history with other types of evidence wherever possible.

In my time, we established an oral history group to record Centerville history. There were usually several people in the room to corroborate the stories. Photos, newspaper articles and other documentation was usually provided.

Some stories that were collected were sensitive in nature, especially the more-recent ones, because participants were still alive, sometimes even sitting in the room. Or there may have been scandals involved. The group was able to talk about people and events, but some of the tragedy and scandals, the so-called "rest of the story" had to be left out of the narrative. I often wondered what percentage the "rest of the story" was. I estimated from some of the stories at our oral history meetings that I knew a lot about that—even a quarter of what really happened was not mentioned. An important reason, if not the key reason for my mission, was to clear up my understanding of my past often based largely on oral history.

Centerville for Christina represented a more-simple and perhaps more-primitive existence than she had experienced during the first 25 years of her life. Born in a small village near Dresden, she would have seen Dresden in its glory with its churches, museums and castles. Christina would have seen other large cities like Bremen from whence she sailed. She would have seen the vast Atlantic Ocean from a large ship. And she would have seen New York City, America's largest city, when she arrived in 1848.

In Centerville, however, Christina would never see a building taller than two stories for the rest of her life. She would see log, wood frame and brick structures, but no fancy stone or block buildings. She would never see Milwaukee, sixty miles away. Christina would also never learn much of the language of her new country.

I got the impression that Christina loved Friedrich more than she ever loved Alfred. Alfred's arrival was certainly timely and advantageous for her. But Alfred often preferred the company of Shelbina Kaiser, known as Shelby, the neighbor woman for whom he had conducted her marriage to Wilhelm Kaiser in his role as Justice of The Peace. Shelby made home-brewed beer that Alfred sometimes drank in excess.

Christina would get sadder as the years went on. The afore-mentioned losses were only the beginning of her sorrows. The scandal with her father's divorce and the pregnant maid negatively impacted her early life. Christina and Gustav left their father and moved with their mother to Meissen, a larger city in Saxony. Then Christina and Gustav left their mother behind in Saxony to move to America, never to see her again. By the time Christina died of a stroke at 71, she would have lost two husbands, three sons, three daughters, one grandson and one daughter-in-law.

Another granddaughter, born in the Wagner house and six years old when Christina died, told me that Christina never smiled and always wore black clothing. She said that Christina was knitting one Saturday and suddenly slumped over in her chair. She had suffered a stroke. Christina would survive until Sunday evening. Well-wishers stopped over after church to see her for what turned out to be the last time.

Mourning women traditionally wore black, sometimes up to a year. Christina had little opportunity or reason between the frequent deaths in her life to change into more-colorful clothes.

Christina, as I would know her during my mission, was generally quiet, but could be opinionated. Most of my conversations with Christina tended to be brief. I could not get much additional information out of her about her past. She did say that her family scandal was unforgivable but gave no other details. As much as she may have often missed Saxony, she had finally moved on, she would later maintain.

It was a tremendous relief for me to know what Christina and Alfred really looked like. Over a century later, we had only two possible photographs of Christina, one in doubt and the other disputed with another family's ancestor. In the end, neither photo seemed to make sense. This was confirmed when I finally met her.

One of the descendants of Christina's brother Gustav, not knowing who was pictured in her collection of old Freiburg photos, would one day throw all of them in a burn pile and then phone to offer me the prayer books. "The photos had no names, so they were of no use to anyone," she would say. I was devastated.

We would also never find a photograph of Alfred. He told me during my mission that he had never been photographed.

CHAPTER 12 – ALFRED

Elsa began to talk about a woman friend from the community named Nanette Graber who she was close to.

"Is she married?" I asked.

"No. You'll meet her sometime."

Elsa suddenly gazed toward the road. Alfred and Hugo were on their way home.

I watched intently as Alfred came up to the house. He was a smaller man than I expected, given that some of his children would be tall in stature. I could see in him the Wagner face, especially the prominent nose that many of his male descendants would have. I also have that nose. Alfred's demeanor seemed deliberate, his steps measured, his movement exhibiting a sense of caution.

We shook hands. I held his hand tightly, as if to securely link myself to my past. He was surprised to see me, of course. After brief introductions, Alfred confessed that he knew nothing of my surname nor my relationship to him in Lippe, but quickly seemed to accept my initial story. "I have met several relatives in my past that I didn't know

I had," he admitted.

Alfred seemed to like me immediately. I breathed a sigh of relief, having gotten past major hurtles with the fake story of my past and in being accepted by both the Wagners and Elsa.

Alfred invited me to stay for supper, then escorted me on horseback back to Hika that evening. He heartily invited me back to the farm the next day. He promised to find me a place to stay in the neighborhood and give me some temporary work and meals.

We talked extensively over the next few days. I could never let on, of course, that I knew anything about Alfred's past or future, the family, or the farm. Yet I could hardly hide my enthusiasm to find out more about the Wagners and the farm.

Alfred did not further question my background, perhaps saving it for another day. Like Elsa, he hungered for conversation from beyond the borders of Centerville. He was a man of the world, ever curious, ever respectful. I must have gotten some of his genes!

Alfred related to me that he was forced to leave the future Germany when he was 30 years old. It was not his original intention to move to America. Alfred got caught up in a dispute, fought a pistol duel in Lippe in 1847, and killed his opponent. He may have won the duel and the dispute that went with it, and saved his life, of course. But in the process, he lost his homeland. Dueling was illegal by that time, a capital crime. In order to escape his fate, Alfred fled across a border hidden in a coffin carried by his friends and then fled to America.

I already knew most of the story, but only from one source. No one in the oral history of our immediate family knew or said anything about the duel, only that Alfred had done something serious. We heard about the duel from cousins in Missouri.

Alfred came to America on a Dutch ship with a false passport. Once in New York, he resumed using his real name. We knew more than a century later that he was indeed Alfred Wagner because we still have a prayer book from Germany with his name on it. We never found a passport.

Alfred worked in New York City for six months, learned English and saved some money. He heard about land in Wisconsin, coming to Sheboygan in late 1848. His friend, Meister, who came with him from New York, decided to go on to Milwaukee. Alfred, however, decided to stay in the area. He headed north toward Centerville.

I had heard from other relatives that Alfred was offered temporary lodging at a village later called Erdmann northwest of Sheboygan. Erdmann was named after one of my father's wealthy uncles who owned several businesses in the village.

Alfred declined the invitation to stay in Erdmann, declaring that he knew where he was going. He arrived on foot at Gustav Freiburg's farm looking for work. Gustav, whose sister Christina next door had recently become a widow, suggested that Alfred help her out. He did and they would soon marry.

Alfred always wanted to return to his homeland for a visit but risked being arrested for his crime. He was a German nationalist who wanted the German states to be united into one country. He would get his wish before he died when Otto von Bismarck, a Prussian, united the Germans in early 1871.

The family story was that Alfred died of homesickness for Germany. That was not likely the real cause, but a contributing factor. As I got to know Alfred better, it was true that he longed for Germany and may have even wanted to move back. Like many immigrants, he was never fully American. He had one foot planted in America and the other foot still firmly planted in the old country.

Alfred grew up in a glassmaking family in Lippe-Detmold. He left a substantial inheritance behind in Lippe that he was never able to claim. Alfred showed me a glass cup the family used as a "spooner" with a fancy "W" etched on it. He had made it himself in Detmold and brought it with him. A spooner was used to keep spoons in on the kitchen table. The family still kept a spooner on the table when I was growing up. It appeared that Alfred was reminiscing about his past when he brought his spooner out for me to look at.

In later years, only my father's oldest sister claimed to remember the spooner. It may have eventually been broken from use and discarded. Or it may have passed on to other descendants and lost to history. Although I never expect to ever find it, in my mind it serves as a kind of holy grail for the Wagner family. It is perhaps ironic that the city I lived in later in life was called Spooner.

Because of his northwestern German dialect, the local Saxons occasionally commented about Alfred's German. "He spoke funny," one of my older relatives had said. Although Alfred spoke reasonable Saxon German by the time that I met him, he would sometimes slip back into his distinct Lippe dialect when talking to me. This was a problem for me, because of course, I really wasn't a Lipper. I understood him well enough but insisted on talking to him in the more-common High German of the time.

Alfred was not part of the shipload of immigrants that arrived in Sheboygan County from Lippe-Detmold in 1847 and who founded the Mission House Seminary, now Lakeland College, in the northwestern part of the county. There was no indication in our oral history that he ever had any contact with them, neither in Europe nor here, even though they settled less than fifteen miles apart. Alfred eventually told me that he met them once, had a nice conversation, and left it at that. Although Alfred was religious, he may have been uncomfortable with the more conservative Mission House crowd.

The one meeting with the Lippers that Alfred had occurred when he joined his Leitner neighbors to take a wagonload of grain to Sheboygan Falls, twenty miles away, to be ground into flour. Some of the Mission people who lived about ten miles from there were also in town.

The Leitners left the farm just after midnight, picked up Alfred on their way south, arrived in Sheboygan Falls at mid-day, got the grain ground, and then returned to Centerville by midnight, a twenty-two-hour ordeal with horses and wagon. Today such a trip by car or truck would take a half hour one way. After a flour mill was built in Hika a year later, the long trip to Sheboygan Falls was no longer necessary.

Over the next several days, Alfred confirmed much of what I had learned a century later and added several details. The duel was both personal and political, fought over a long-standing dispute with a business competitor and supporter of the ruling class.

Alfred's choice of Centerville was sheer happenstance. He was tired of traveling, did not want to live in a city, and liked what he saw of the Centerville shoreline from the ship. The topography and vegetation of Centerville reminded him of his homeland, Alfred would tell me. After some deliberation, he got off at Sheboygan, the next stop. Alfred would lose contact with his friend Meister and never see him again.

I asked Alfred about his job as Justice of The Peace. He liked it, he admitted, but I knew he would give it up in a few more years. "It gives me a sense of responsibility for the community," he admitted. "I feel like I'm paying my debt for the stupid things I did in Lippe. What I don't like is that the locals, with their intention to be respectful, want to address me as 'Justice Sir' or 'Mister Wagner'. I keep telling them to just call me 'Herr Wagner' or just 'Alfred'. I especially hate to be called 'Mister' because it means 'manure handler' in German!" Alfred joked.

CHAPTER 13 – HELPING

I helped the Wagners as much as possible, even though I was finding occasional outside work for cash. The Wagner tasks included clearing more forest land, making firewood, butchering, plowing, finishing the barn, planting an apple orchard, and building fences. The work was incredibly hard. Even though I grew up on a dairy farm, this very farm, in fact, the work was never this grueling! It gave me considerable respect for the effort that went into building the farm that I inherited when I briefly took over the operation when I got out of college.

I especially hated the butchering. The sight of blood flowing out of the animal made me queasy. I once even passed out. Everyone on the scene, including Elsa, laughed. Being a doctor or veterinarian would never be part of my future!

I hated the loud squeal of the dying pig. "Can't you tranquillize the poor beast?" I asked.

"What do you mean?" Alfred asked.

"Why don't you feed the pig some whiskey or vodka, get it drunk, and then kill it? I've seen it done."

"Why waste good whiskey on a pig!" Hugo shouted. I never heard anything about Hugo from my knowledge of Wagner history. I discovered that I did not like his crudeness and criticism, and never got along with him very well.

But Alfred, considering my comment, agreed with me. "We ought to try that the next time. Does it affect the meat?"

"Not enough to matter," I replied. I wanted to say but didn't, that the adrenaline produced by the panicked pig, added to the testosterone in an uncastrated boar, would have had much more of a negative effect on the taste of the meat than any pint of booze. However, It wouldn't do for me to talk about hormones that weren't discovered yet.

During my long shifts doing manual labor, I often wished that the settlers would have had modern tools and machinery. At least a chain saw, for Gods' sake! But again, I stopped myself from talking about things that were not yet invented at the risk changing the future. Nonetheless, I always thought about ways that would make life easier for them. This same thought process was useful when I had worked with farmers in my time in less-developed places overseas. In Centerville, I sometimes managed to drive the local blacksmiths crazy with my new-fangled ideas.

I didn't like chopping or sawing firewood as much as I liked splitting it. I spent hours at the Wagners splitting firewood on top of a stump. Before splitting, we had to first saw logs into pieces not longer than fifteen inches so that they would fit into the stove. I didn't know at the time that another stump on the farm would become an important part of my visit as a consistent meeting place for Elsa and me.

"Wonderful!" Alfred said, remarking on my enthusiasm as I split a particularly tough piece of wood right down the middle. "You can split as much wood as you like. Just remember, it is easier to split it top to bottom, just like the leaves fall."

A very positive part of my experience with Alfred was that he was easy to work for. His attitude always was that, as much as he missed his origins, he could have been stuck in Lippe, either on the losing end of the duel, in jail, serving long military duty or struggling against the royalty whom he thoroughly disliked.

For someone who had fought a duel, Alfred was something of a pacifist. He did not seem like the type of person who would jump at a chance to pick up a gun. I was hoping to get more details about what led up to the duel, but Alfred soon kept deflecting questions about it. However, the incident seemed to have increased his respect for all life in general.

The Lippers had served under Napoleon and lost many men to his cause, particularly on the failed Russian front. "Lippers were tired of war," Alfred would say more than once. His father fought and survived but came back with physical and mental problems. I agreed with Alfred's assessment, inventing more stories about my non-existent Lipper past.

"When do people start rebelling against it all, like they did in Europe?" I asked Alfred one day.

"When too many of them are poor or hungry or abused, and then something sets them off," he replied. "There's a point when the problems get to be too much."

"There's a tipping point?" I asked.

"Sure."

"Can you predict it?" I continued.

"Hard to say," Alfred said, "but can you feel when it's coming. Maybe it's when the kings and their friends have all the money."

"Who starts the rebellion?" I asked.

"Often young men, full of passion and fury, sometimes a small group of rebels with guns. Sometimes it's the army itself. At times, people just go into the streets without guns and get shot. But it usually starts something."

"Farmers or city folk?"

"Not sure," Alfred said, "but when times are tough, it's usually the city people that go into the streets. In tough times, farmers just work harder. To preserve one's reign, I guess, the ruler needs to keep bread cheap for the city folk, but one can always keep squeezing the farmers. It's not fair."

"When the logging on the farm is finished, do you think you can make living from farming?" I asked Alfred, changing the subject.

"Not with the prices of wheat and barley as they are now. People are saying if we get a war, Wisconsin may have to feed the army. That should help the price of wheat some. Soldiers always need to eat," Alfred said.

"We need to produce more meat, milk and cheese," I said, "prophesying the future of Wisconsin."

Chapter 14 – Farming

The Wagners owned two horses, two oxen, three "milch" cows, five sheep, five "swine", and several chickens and turkeys. These provided ample food, draft power and some income.

There was small income from the sale of rye, wheat and barley. All Centerville farmers grew rye and there was a good demand for it, but most of it stayed on the farm. Rye was an important crop because the straw was commonly used with mud for insulation in building walls, bedding and sometimes for thatched roofs. The straw was also used for making baskets and beehives. Rye seed was ground into flour. Germans loved their rye bread.

The main sources of income for the Wagners, and most farmers in the area in 1858, however, were wood products, mainly timber, firewood, and shingles. Farmers would make shingles during the long winter nights when they had to be indoors anyway.

The larger animals all had names. One horse was named Nancy, interestingly, as it also was the same name as my father's last horse as well as my youngest sister.

"Why Nancy?" I asked Alfred.

"I visited the City of Nancy in Alsace-Lorraine once with my uncle on family business," Alfred replied. "I really liked the city. It is now controlled by France. But I think that Lorraine should be a German state," he added, betraying his German nationalism.

I noticed that the Wagners did not have a dog. "You need a watchdog," I told Alfred.

"Why don't you find me one?" he suggested.

Working with Alfred, I learned a lot about the trees of the time. They were virgin growth, often incredibly large. Green ash was very abundant in the area. Some pine trees were so wide that two of their logs would not have fit side-by-side on a future railroad car, one Freiburg descendant once told me. Seeing the gigantic pines with my own eyes, it confirmed what he had said.

Moving the logs was extremely difficult. Teams of oxen or horses were used to pull logs. There were no large rivers in the area on which to float logs. There was no railroad yet. Lake Michigan was only three miles away and downhill, yet there was no good way to move large logs or large-cut timbers even a few miles. It was soon realized that it was easier to bring the sawmill to the farm than to transport the logs to the sawmill.

Alfred observed that cutting into a forest on the north or west edge could result in wind damage to exposed inward trees. Broken or cracked trunks greatly reduced their value for timber. "I don't need that much firewood," Alfred joked. "The windward trees," he suggested, "grew up accustomed to bending with the wind as they grew. They became stronger, serving as weather sentinels for the rest of the forest."

The immigrant Germans practiced types of silviculture. They pruned lower branches from younger trees to promote straight saw-logs as the trees grew taller. Sugar maples were tapped to make maple syrup. Alfred and I talked a lot about trees.

"What happens when all the trees are gone?" I asked Alfred again, always prying to see what he envisioned of the future. I remembered seeing photos of Centerville from the early 1900s that looked very devoid of trees.

"I haven't thought about it," he replied. "We'll have more farmland, I guess. Hopefully the crop acres will replace the income from timber."

"I was thinking more about the environment," I thought to myself, realizing that the idea of preserving the environment was not in the public conscience at the time.

"So does a lack of trees change the weather, the wildlife, and the soil?" I asked.

Alfred thought for a moment and said that he didn't know about changes to the weather from deforestation, but that it was an interesting idea.

"What did you see when trees were removed in Europe?" I asked.

"It took Europeans centuries to conquer the land," Alfred continued, implying that people needed clearing and farming to survive. "There is a balance," he continued. "We need both trees and open land. Parts of this farm won't be tilled. Look at the southwest part of the farm over there," he said pointing. "It is too hilly. We will always want to have trees for firewood and building. Even hunting," he laughed. "Even just walking in the woods for fun!"

"Have you seen any wolves or bears?" I asked.

"Just a few black bears" Alfred replied. "The wolves were here, but settlers either shot them or the wolves just moved away."

"What about deer?"

"Some," he said.

I knew that deer would eventually be gone from the Centerville area, at least until the 1930s when they would start returning from the north as trees returned to the landscape. My father would see his first deer on the farm in 1934. Bears would be absent from the county for over a hundred years.

I commented on the rich, deep topsoil. "Kewaunee silt loam," I said.

"Is that what they call it?" Alfred asked.

"Most of it will be gone someday," I said.

"How?" he asked.

Realizing that I was giving away something about the future of the farm and farming in general, I asked Alfred about the topsoil that was left in Europe.

"You're right," he said, "we manage to farm most of it away somehow."

"Tillage is a major culprit," I said. "It results in erosion."

"How could we grow crops without tillage?" Alfred asked.

"Plowing is very destructive," I lamented. "You especially don't want to leave your soil bare over the winter. Spring tillage is an option. There are ways to seed without disturbing the soil too much."

"The problem is that we don't have enough time in the spring to plow," Alfred replied. "Where there is clay, you just can't break it up in the spring. It just gets hard and lumpy."

"We'll talk about this later," I replied.

The Wagner farm had its fair share of rocks, which we called stones in my time. Before and after the soil was tilled, we had to remove stones of various sizes. We used horses and a wagon to pick the smaller ones. Some stones were too large to lift into a wagon. Alfred built a sled of planks we called a "stone boat" to drag around with the horses. It was easy to roll the larger stones onto the stone boat.

Some farmers built stone fences around the fields. Alfred decided to make a large stone pile behind the barn.

"I will need these stones someday for building, so I don't want to have them too far away," Alfred said.

"Good idea!" I agreed.

Alfred was right. Later the stones would be used for the basement of the new house including the cistern, for the understory or basement of a new barn, and for one of the first vertical silos built in the township. "It is easier to make fences out of posts and rails," he said. "It is certainly easier to move wooden fences if I decide to change the layout of my fields."

"I like you," Alfred said to me one day. "You seem to have a grasp of things, of the larger world, like someone who senses and understands what is going to happen."

"Thank you," I replied. "I always like to look at the bigger picture!"

CHAPTER 15 – SETTLING

Alfred was not able to offer me more than food and a little cash in exchange for my labor. I did not mind. Within the first month after my arrival, I found paying work at a local harness and blacksmith shop down the road, about a half mile from the Wagner farm. Not liking blacksmithing, I spent most of my time dealing with harnesses. It was not fulltime work, but the hours were enough to pay my bills. More than a century later I would work as a mechanic for a winter in that same building.

I was able to get time off for neighborhood projects, especially in the summer for harvesting. I especially liked helping with masonry and building construction. I made cash doing those too, although I continued to support Wagner's in-kind labor trade with the neighbors. Hugo, the hired man, had moved on to another job, so I was much needed.

The Hessels did offer me a room in their log house. They had finished the new frame house and moved in. Their hired man and another worker from the neighborhood lived in the log house, as well as a new immigrant couple building a place of their own. Conveniently, I lived a half mile from work and just across the road from the Wagners.

Christina was pregnant again. She would have another son, this one named Otto. The Wagners denied naming him after me. It was a common name of the time that they liked, I was told, not a family name or sponsor's name. I knew that the Wagners did have a relative or two named Otto in Europe. However, the thought that an ancestral member of a family could be named after a descendant member was an intriguing idea!

I never liked the name Otto when I was growing up. It was really my middle name. All the Ottos in the community were either old or dead. When grade-schoolers found out what my middle name was, they made fun of me by calling me Otto. I hated it, but the name stuck and became my moniker in later years.

I was spending a lot of time with Elsa. It seemed that we couldn't resist being together. We never ran out of things to talk about. We enjoyed each other's company.

Elsa had a few suitors before, but her independence, intellect, even quirkiness, were too much for them. Elsa worried about being a spinster yet wouldn't concede an inch to the usual male authority.

I nonetheless tried to be non-committal with Elsa, knowing that my stay was temporary. I was initially planning to stay only a few months. Then it became a year. Now it looked like I would stay longer.

My lack of assertiveness in our relationship, however, seemed to have the effect of increasing my appeal to Elsa. I seemed to fill a void in her life. She filled one in mine. I found myself trying not to fall in love with her. She found herself trying not to fall in love with me.

There was gossip about us in the neighborhood. No problem, I thought, we can handle this. It was better than the malicious gossip I heard from some corners concerning Elsa and Nanette. By dating me, Elsa was telling the world that she was "normal".

Chapter 16 – Lady

Antoinette, the Kaiser grandmother, died not long after I arrived. She was in her 80s. Antoinette went suddenly. She was alive and well one day and gone the next.

Her body was prepared for the funeral and shown at the house as was the practice of the time. Someone quietly joked, "It is better to be seen than to be shown."

As funerals go, there was the usual praise for the deceased with the mourning family and in front of the coffin. Praise at a funeral is always nice, but a little too late for the deceased. "How many times have I wished that some of the praise had been given directly to the person before he or she had died?" I commented softly to Elsa.

One of the older neighbors I talked to said, "Who among us will be the next one in the coffin?" Ironically, he died about a month later and was himself the next one in the coffin.

We attended the funeral service in front of the house next to a small walnut tree that Antoinette had planted from a seed she had brought over from Saxony. Several Kaiser descendants over the next century would be married under that tree.

No outside pallbearers were requested. Antoinette had six grand-sons, all big, strong men, who would fulfill the requirement.

Antoinette certainly deserved the praise. She was known to be a real lady. Antoinette was very dignified, very polite, always wise. She also spoke French. She insisted on being called Antoinette, not "Toni" or "Nettie" or some other contraction of the day.

There was talk that Antoinette was a blueblood, an aristocrat, some-how related to a real "Kaiser." She denied it, but her frequent references to European high society made her even more intriguing. Alfred said that she was an entertaining storyteller, even if there was no evidence that she was a member of the upper class. "Some people just take an interest in the affairs of high society," Alfred said.

Later in the day, after Elsa and I had returned home, the Kaiser sons walked solemnly as they accompanied the coffin on a wagon to the cem-etery, passing the Wagner farm. Elsa and I stood near the road in solemn reverence. It was incredibly quiet with the only sounds the clopping of the horse's feet and the shuffling of walking men.

Even the birds went quiet seemingly out of respect. It was as if the entire world recognized the passing of a significant person. The sight of six strong men quietly escorting their grandmother the half mile to her final resting place is something I would never forget.

The rest of the family and several neighborhood mourners, includ-ing Alfred and Christina, and Gustav and Natalie Freiburg, followed a few minutes behind on foot. The rest of the mourners arrived at the cem-etery with horses and buggies. Elsa and I did not go to the cemetery.

"Death is the great equalizer," Elsa stated, after the mourners had passed. "The rich and the poor, the powerful and the weak, the good and the bad, the old and the young, are all brought down in the end to the same fate. The thing that is missing in life is justice."

"That's why there is a God," Elsa concluded after a moment of silence.

"You may be right," I added. "One thing is for sure," I continued. "All our actions are tempered by the reality of imminent death, and if they aren't, they should be. Those in positions to make decisions that directly impact the fate of others should not take that responsibility lightly." I was thinking of the many soldiers and civilians led to their deaths by the whims of selfish and ambitious leaders.

Chapter 17 – Coming

"What was Saxony like?" I asked Elsa one day.

"It was beautiful!" she replied. "I saw mountains in the south. I saw wonderful churches and castles and shops, especially in Dresden and Leipzig. Houses were made of stone and beautifully-painted wood. There were orchestras and choirs with heavenly music. People wore colorful clothes. America is so plain and dull by comparison," Elsa lamented.

"Why did your family leave?" I asked.

"People were unhappy with the kings," Elsa continued. "Some wanted to overthrow the monarchies. There was a failed revolution. Opponents were put in prison. One of them was my uncle. We were tired of being ruled by one country one decade and another the next. We were tired of their wars. People couldn't worship the way they wanted. There was a lot of cold weather. Crops were often failing. The economy was bad. Businesses were failing. Some people were homeless and hungry. My family wanted a better life. These are the same reasons that others I have talked to have given, whether they were German,

Bohemian, Polish or something else."

"There were dealers offering good prices for land in America, some even specifically for Wisconsin," Elsa recalled. "When the kings decided to let people leave rather than continue to subdue them, we went."

"Did you pay for your farm before coming here?" I asked.

"No, some family members came before we did. They held the land for us. Some people paid a lot of money to unscrupulous dealers in Europe for land in America, only to find nothing when they came here. We didn't trust those people."

I pondered over the many reasons Elsa mentioned for leaving Europe. There were obviously many so-called "push" factors. There were also "pull" factors like the cheap land, more "lebensraum" (space to live in), and the many opportunities and freedoms America had to offer.

One important factor was simply the ability to leave. More and more sailing ships were crossing the Atlantic up to the mid-1800s. Then the steamship industry started to flourish. One could cross the ocean in less than a week on a steamship as compared to ten weeks on a sailing vessel. There was plenty of competition between shipping companies, driving prices down. The development of railroads and canals on both sides of the ocean also reduced travel time and cost.

Europeans who left in the mid-1800s missed much of the European version of the industrial revolution, often unkind to common laborers, but they also missed an incredible period of intellectual enlightenment.

America had its own industrial revolution and enlightenment period too. The rush for land made farmers out of many first-generation immigrants. The second generation, running out of land, either moved farther north or west or entered the industrial work-force.

Germans came to Wisconsin to settle, to put down roots, not to exploit and then move on. Germans were peaceful. They did not bring gangs or a mafia with them.

As Elsa and I continued the discussion about immigration, I added the idea that America was a safe haven for misfits. The combination of monarchial and religious societies of Europe were for centuries extremely hard on minorities, free-thinkers and geniuses. That is why so many writers, scientists and artists were stifled, forced to recant or went running across borders. There was torture and execution. Thousands of so-called heretics and witches were killed.

"What about the voyage to America?" I asked Elsa.

"The land trip to Bremen was long. We had to pass through kingdoms that didn't like us. People tried to charge us too much for food and lodging. Sometimes we could not understand their language. We were so afraid that we would run out of money before we even got to America. Fortunately, we had a man traveling with us who knew the way. He was a type of travel agent who spoke German, French, Dutch and English. He negotiated all our fares including the ship. He told us all the prices and what he would make for himself. People thought he was reasonable. Everything he told us turned out to be true. We were lucky, I guess."

"We had to stay in Bremen for a few days to wait for the ship," Elsa continued. "Most of the captains were not nice, I was told. We had a good one. He tried his best to make us comfortable. But the ship was cold and dark. I loved the sea at first. Then when I could no longer see land, I cried for my homeland. Most of the ships in 1848 were sailing ships that took nine or more weeks to reach America. The Freiburgs, Hessels, Meyers, and other neighbors all came on sailing ships."

"My trip was on a steamer which took just over a week," I commented.

"You were lucky," Elsa replied.

"Some of us who are fortunate may have a chance to go back for a visit, but I am sure that I will never see my birthplace again," Elsa moaned. "Oh, how I miss my friends! I miss my grandmother Kune who was so kind! I miss my uncle Gustav who used to tell me such interesting stories. He was a merchant who traveled all over Europe. Those two always wrote me letters. Then my grandmother died. My uncle was killed in an accident while riding a horse. I stare at the last letters they ever wrote to me and wonder what it would have been like had I stayed."

"Kune?" I asked. "What kind of name is that?"

"Kunegunda," she laughed. "Funny name for a woman, isn't it? From the East, maybe Polish."

"Some names are just not meant to come back!" I thought.

"What did the Saxons think about you and others leaving for America?" I asked.

"Families were torn," Elsa replied. "Many people were angry. Some argued that America was full of wild animals and savage tribes. Others blessed us, saying that it was time to look for new opportunities. In the end, there had to be an acceptance of the new reality. But there was a lot of sadness. Despite vague assurances about trying to return to Europe for a visit after the promise of America would make people wealthy, most families would never see each other again. The worst problem is that, although I can see opportunities ahead, we are hardly any better off here in America than we were in Europe."

"It is so hard!" Elsa almost shouted. She welled up in tears.

"The ocean was boring at first," Elsa continued after a few moments. "Then the waves made me sick. I could not eat for two days. One of the crew liked me and offered some of his own food. The ship provided food as part of the passage, but it was never enough and not very good. I told him that I could not take it without sharing with my family. He told me stories about crossing the ocean and the interesting people he had met. He even had a map of the world. He was nice."

"But one of the other crew members kept touching me," Elsa continued. "I was only 13 years old. I was about to tell my father or the captain. However, I didn't need to. I hit him in the face! He didn't bother me anymore."

"How was New York?" I asked.

"The place was called Castle Garden," Elsa said. "The immigration agents were not nice. They could not spell our names and didn't seem to care. They asked many questions, like do you have any diseases, did you commit any crimes? Why would anyone say yes?"

Castle Garden would have been the same port facility of entry for me, had I not been lying about my origin. I never brought it up to Elsa because I would not have been able to describe it. Main entry locations for Germans coming to America that I was aware of included New York, Philadelphia, New Orleans and Montreal. One of my ancestors came through Baltimore.

"I saw them reject a man," Elsa lamented. "They decided to send him back. His whole family went back with him. As much as we all sometimes doubted our decision, I couldn't imagine going back to face the people I had left. I saw a woman whom they thought was sick. I was told they put her in a hospital with a fence around it."

"I was happy to get out of New York," Elsa continued. "It took us three weeks to arrive here, first up to Albany on the river, then through the Erie canal, and then through the Great Lakes. It was a nice, peaceful trip. We were now in America. For three weeks we were finally able to talk about the future and stop worrying about getting here."

I asked Elsa about the letters, passports and other documents that she and the Wagners had. Except for the deeds, no letters or passports would survive to my time.

After a couple of decades, the Wagners never looked back. Until my aunt returned to Germany a hundred years later with her husband who served in World War II, and then my sister and I in the later part of the 20th Century, no direct descendants ever went back.

CHAPTER 18 – POLKA

Elsa loved dancing much more than I did. I was a real klutz on the dance floor. Elsa promised to teach me. I got the impression that she wanted to show me off.

Dances and church were the two main public places with a lot of people around to show off one's partner. Dancing further strengthened our relationship, both in reality and in the eyes of the public.

Polka dancing was the popular pastime of the day. No worthwhile wedding would be held without a polka dance. Of course, I didn't dance well at first, stepping on Elsa's toes, but the music was wonderful, and the camaraderie was delightful!

It was the Bohemians who gave us the polka. They had the best orchestras. We saw a new Bohemian group in Manitowoc County in 1858 featuring a magnificent clarinet player. He was the son of another orchestra leader in the community. His music had a faster tempo. His was no ordinary oompah band. Only the best dancers could keep up. Couples would hop in unison off the floor. I heard of a contest where couples had to polka over a jump rope.

The Saxons lived next to the Bohemians in Europe. They were geographically separated by a small mountain range called the Elsters. Ethnically different, Saxons were largely Germans and Bohemians were largely of Slavic origin. The future Czech Republic, the home of Bohemians, also contained a large group of ethnic Germans. The two largest ethnic groups in Manitowoc County in 1858 were Germans, who dominated the southern part of the county, and Bohemians who dominated the northern part. One could feel a kinship between the two groups in the 1850s and even in the 1950s.

A third nationality located east of the Saxons and Bohemians in Europe, the Poles, had their own brand of polka music. Newton, the township north of Centerville, featured a Polish settlement. They were frequent attendees at Centerville dances. Elsa took me to some of the Polish dances. There was a warmth between the three communities in Manitowoc County that was delightful, something that would probably not have existed in Europe.

What I liked about the dances was that, apart from church, these were the social events that mattered. Polkas and waltzes brought people together, no matter what their backgrounds. There were Protestants and Catholics, Whigs and Democrats, Germans, Bohemians and Poles, of course, and even a few Irish and Norwegians from the area.

The dance menu of the day also included "landlers" and "schottisches." The instruments of the time included an accordion or concertina, bass, double horn or tuba, clarinet, drum, and piano when available.

At one of the dances, the orchestra introduced a new polka. It was called the "Elsa" Polka. "See Elsa," I stated. "They named a polka after you!" It would become our favorite. Elsa would share "her polka" with other dancers too, often getting an applause when it was played.

Men who would drink too much and get rowdy could find themselves on the receiving end of the famous Centerville bouncer, a six-foot, six-inch, 450-pound fellow named Gordy. I once saw him grab two young men by the collars, one with each arm, lift them up, and carry them out. His regular job was working in a livery stable, shoeing horses and other tasks. People said that no horse and no drunkard ever got the best of him.

Elsa could be a real dance celebrity when she wanted to. All the young men wanted to dance with her as if it were a kind of challenge, both to match her on the dance floor and for bragging rights. Unmarried suitors were always in the hunt. But at the end of the day, Elsa and I were the ones everyone was talking about. Jealous young men taunted me about my odd culture, my language, my perceived intellectualism, my lack of a tough exterior and my shortage of dance skills. They did or said anything they could think of to respectfully scare me away. Throughout it all, I maintained a sense of poise and humor.

There was one dance where I encountered a more serious threat. One fellow who told me that I should stay away from Elsa challenged me to join him in a fist fight in the parking lot. I refused, of course, and started to walk away. He grabbed me by the suspenders and threw me on the floor. He was joined by a few of his fellow taunters. Before I could get up, Elsa went after the man with her fists. A Polish man whom I had not met before intervened to help me and Elsa. He got between Elsa and the offender. Gordy then arrived and landed his fist to the offender's face, knocking him out cold. Gordy then told the rest of the rowdies to remove the unconscious man and leave the premises. They did. We thanked the Pole in English for his assistance and bought him a beer.

Polka dances were the venues where many couples met and where some couples sometimes broke up. One of Elsa's friends ended her relationship at a dance. It was not a pretty scene. There was an intense argument. After it was over, her boyfriend took another woman home that night. He would eventually marry her.

Elsa and I took her friend home. That dance hall, now part of a residence, still exists today. "The marriage would not have worked anyway,"

Alfred later said. "They were about as compatible as oil and water."

At one dance, Elsa introduced me to a very handsome, young man whom she was obviously fond of. I had seen him before, but Elsa never mentioned him. He had an unforgettable name "Magnus." Elsa told me he was studying for the priesthood. She admitted to me that she would have liked to date him. But there were the obvious obstacles, his celibate profession, his being a Catholic, and Elsa being Elsa.

"It's a shame!" she said about his going into the priesthood. "Nobody will inherit his intelligence and good looks!"

"Maybe you could talk him out of the priesthood and then out of being a Catholic!" I joked.

Chapter 19 – Church

Elsa and I frequently attended church. The Evangelical church that the Wagners attended at the time, like other churches in the area, seemed to me to have inordinate amount of power over people's lives.

Nothing wrong with keeping people moral and saving souls, however, I had trouble with the idea of constantly scaring people to death with the imminent threat of hell or wrath of God, and then telling you that the same God of Love would save you on a mere commitment to Him. Fire and brimstone sermons never went over so well with me and many others in modern times.

I shared some of these thoughts with Elsa. In addition to the issues of salvation, I felt that too many people, caught in the vices of the church and the culture, lived very unfulfilled lives. Too many people were not aspiring high enough. Others, afraid of risks, appeared to be tiptoeing carefully through life to make it safely to death. Where were the scientists, professors, inventors, and innovators going to come from?

Elsa and I both agreed that two positive characteristics of the

Germans were their piousness and devotion to hard work. However, two negative characteristics of the Germans that I saw in Centerville were too much devotion to hard work and not enough devotion to higher thought.

Knowing what innovations were ahead, in fact, just around the corner, I felt a higher priority should be on thinking through rather than just working through challenges. I couldn't understand why so many forces in society, often the most religious, appeared to be afraid of change and kept holding progress back. I suppose my coming from the future made me too impatient with the past, I thought to myself.

After all, America would become "one hell of a success," according to a future Speaker of the House. That success was certainly due in part to the contributions of the Germans, the largest ethnic group in America for a whole century. The scientists, professors and inventors would indeed come, and many from that group.

I asked Elsa why there seemed to be a "tug of war," so to speak, between those in society who craved familiarity and stability, and those who wanted new things, perhaps too quickly.

For once, Elsa didn't have an answer for me. She just said told me to be patient. "We are doing our best," she said as she suddenly patted me on the back.

The minister of the Evangelical church was a nice enough person, almost too simple though. He was all about saying nice things and praising God every chance he got. I felt that he didn't have enough perspective to know how to deal with my soul or even that of Elsa, given our rather questioning and complicated thought processes.

The Lutheran minister, on the other hand, was a true intellectual philosopher of 19th-Century caliber. He was an avid historian, a good violinist and able to speak several languages. It was because of his meticulous recording of information on parishioners who had died that I was able to later trace Christina's origins. He took a more logical and soft approach to saving souls. The minister was a totally boring sermonizer, however, who missed his calling in ivory tower academia. I enjoyed talking with him on those days when he wore his philosophical hat.

The Lutheran minister's second parish featured a new church building that was only walking distance from the Wagner farm. Elsa and I suggested to the Wagners that they switch to this church for convenience's sake. They eventually did so because the Evangelicals built a new church farther away, six miles distant instead of the previous three.

I was happy to attend the church where my father would many years later be baptized. It operated for 60 years until it merged with the church in Cleveland. The shed where the horses were kept during the winter services was removed, half of it becoming the garage for the new church parsonage in Cleveland.

I noticed that the widows usually sat in the left pews and the widowers in the right pews. There was no rule for this, of course, it's just what developed. Pews were not assigned like they were in the Catholic church at the time. In the Lutheran church, the people who thought they were somehow more pious often sat in the front.

"What do you think about Darwin and evolution?" I asked Elsa one day.

"I don't really understand it," she admitted. "But we are not descended from monkeys!"

"What do you think?" she asked.

I didn't want to bring up my complex, 20th-century knowledge of biology. "I think the theory makes good arguments, I replied, but it does not make God and religion invalid. For us to have purpose in our lives, for the world to make sense, there should be a greater intelligence, a greater power out there."

I asked Elsa about one of her Freiburg cousin families who joined a cult and moved to the new state of Oregon. She suddenly stared at me, surprised that I knew about the story, since we had never discussed it.

I had forgotten that my knowledge of this was derived from my later research into family history.

Nonetheless, Elsa continued with the story. "They were told that the world was going to end. They moved to an island to meet Jesus."

"And then?" I asked, already knowing the result.

"They sold or gave away all their possessions. They sat on the island for a week until they ran out of food. Nothing happened. They returned to the mainland, embarrassed. One wrote a letter, stating that most of them had left the group. I doubt they will ever return to Wisconsin," Elsa said.

I didn't say but knew that some of the grandchildren would one day come back to visit.

"What did Jesus say?" I said. "Only God knows when the last day will be."

CHAPTER 20 – AGNOSTIC

I saw an older widower at some of the dances. He sat in the corner most of the time just smiling as he watched the twirling couples. There were some widows present, but no one would dance with him. His name was Ferdinand and he did not attend any church.

Every community had an individual or family that, for whatever reason, would not attend church. They were often the objects of scorn or pity.

"He's an atheist," someone said of Ferdinand.

"Going straight to hell!" Christina would say.

Alfred would tell Christina not to play God. "You don't know his story. I've done business with the man," he said. "He is totally honest and generous. Pays what he owes before leaving the premises. Never committed any crime either. Better citizen than some of the Christians around here."

Elsa asked me what I thought. "I agree with Alfred," I said. "We should not judge him. Maybe he believes in God, but not in religion? This is America," I added. "He should have the right to believe as he wishes."

"Have you ever talked to him?" I asked Elsa.

"No, but I am curious about his beliefs. I will go to see him some time," I said.

"I will go with you," Elsa replied.

"No, I don't want you to be seen with him," I said. "People will accuse you. For myself, I don't care. I can defend my reputation."

"You are brave," Elsa said.

One day I did visit Ferdinand. He was from East Prussia. His family had moved to Saxony when he was nine.

"I was brought up Christian, but I'm part Jewish," he admitted. "My Jewish ancestors were persecuted by Christians. That's why we moved. I don't like hard-headed Christians, although I know most of them mean well. I married one, after all. I do believe there is a God, but He is certainly not Christian."

"Jews are often accused of being unscrupulous businessmen," I asked.

"They are no less scrupulous than Christian businessmen, just more successful," he said. "Jews, wherever they lived in Europe, were forced into a corner. They were not allowed to own land. They had to live in cities. They were not allowed to vote or run for office. They were often not given jobs. They were not given loans. Jews had to pool their resources, bank their own money and obtain higher education to get ahead."

"What about the argument that Jews murdered Jesus?" I asked.

"Jesus was Jew, one of them," he replied. "There was a power struggle among the Jewish sects. Jesus brought a new way of thinking. He offered new hope for eternity. Jesus was a hero to many of the common people, but a threat to the ruling order, both Jewish and Roman. The religious and political establishment of the time were the ones that killed Jesus. It had nothing to do with being a Jew."

"How did you come here?" I asked.

"I married a Saxon, of course. We came to America for many of the same reasons that the others came."

"What were some of the reasons?" I asked.

Ferdinand mentioned several. "People left Europe because of political and economic chaos, war, long military conscriptions, escape from family scandals, escape after committing a crime, freedom from the tyranny of the kings. Reasons for coming to America included democracy, less government control, ease of starting a business, better standard of living, freedom from crime, freedom to practice a different religion, or freedom from religion itself."

"Is that enough?" Ferdinand asked with a sigh. "I could probably think of more reasons."

I looked around his house. It was full of books. I saw a book by Immanuel Kant printed in English. "You read Kant in English?" I asked Ferdinand in English.

"I was born near Konigsberg," he replied in English himself. "He was one of us. Kant is a tough one to understand. I tried to read him in German, then English, but couldn't figure him out either way," he laughed. "But I like the fact that he puts reason above faith."

I related this to Elsa. "I must read Kant sometime," she laughed. "But I still believe in God and Jesus."

CHAPTER 21 – CHRISTMAS

Christmas was the biggest annual event for most people, ahead of Easter, the Fourth of July and Halloween. Halloween would be more important later and involve considerable playing of pranks in rural areas. In Centerville, the Lutherans did not like the fact that the holiday dedicated to chasing out the devil also fell on the same day as the beginning of Luther's Reformation. So, they ignored the holiday for the most part.

Like other church holidays at the time, Christmas was largely a carryover from Europe with a little added influence from America. Christmas at the Wagners was frugal in nature but did meet much of the usual expectations for the holiday. There was a spruce tree with a few candles and ornaments. There was a wreath on the door. Children's gifts that I saw during my mission included a sled, doll, clothes, toy building blocks, wooden horse, chocolate candy, and a flute. The adults would buy needed clothing for each other, make furniture, and knit blankets, rugs and socks.

Christmas cookies were precious. I was surprised, but not so much, that three or four of the same cookies I saw at the Wagners would be made by my mother a hundred years later. Similarly, I was invited for Christmas in a German home in South America a hundred years later only to find the same recipes there too.

The Wagners usually had a special Christmas meal of pork, mashed potatoes, green beans and apple sauce. Christina's brother Gustav, his wife Natalie, and the Hessels would be invited for another meal on one of the following days.

The usual sausages and cheeses were on hand throughout the year. Summer sausage, liverwurst, blood sausage and headcheese were all made on the farm. The Wagners usually had cheddar, brick or limburger cheese in the house, products of a burgeoning local cheese factory industry. If you could get the Limburger past your nose, it usually tasted okay.

Anything not grown on the farm was considered a luxury that had to be purchased. Plums, pears and apples were available from neighbors. The Kaisers were starting to make maple syrup, another Christmas treat. The Wagners had just started an orchard that wasn't producing yet. Applesauce, canned tomatoes and summer sausage were Wagner staples from the 1860s up to the time when I was growing up.

Applesauce in my time could be served on or with almost anything. We even ate applesauce on pizza. Pizza was not known to the early Wagners.

One year for Christmas, I brought ice cream from Manitowoc. Because it was winter, I did not need to pack it in ice. We kept it outside in a milk can until we ate it. Later I would buy the Wagners a hand-cranked, ice cream maker so they could make it at home.

Another year I found a bottled drink called soda. These treats were much appreciated by the children. The adults liked the tastes but complained that the cold temperature of the ice cream and sweetness of the soda made their infected teeth hurt. The favorite holiday drink was eggnog, laced with brandy for the adults.

My most precious Christmas present for the Wagners turned out to be the new puppy named Sophie. Sophie would be their constant companion, especially for the children. She had a special affinity for me, however, that I couldn't explain. Sophie followed me around on the farm and tried to follow me whenever I left. I would have a future farm dog named Sophie when I was farming who would be my constant companion.

Christmas services at the Lutheran church were special. The singing was so loud that it literally shook the rafters. During one of those services, I thought about Christina's original home church in Saxony that I visited 150 years later. I couldn't let on, of course, that I had seen the church. Christina would certainly have been thrilled to know that her former church in Saxony would continue to survive.

I asked Christina about it one day, when it was built, who founded it and so forth. She mentioned that her ancestors, then Catholic, had founded the church in the late 1500s. She confirmed what I saw when I was there. One of the Latinized surnames on a plaque on the side of the church was indeed a Freiburg.

Chapter 22 – Immigrants

The Wagners kept a type of oil around for aches and pains. It must have been a precursor to liniment as it smelled and felt very similar to the real thing I grew up with.

"Where did you get the stuff?" I asked.

"I bought it from a snake oil salesman," Alfred replied. "They come around every now and then with a wagonload of soaps, oils and other concoctions or elixirs. You never know if you can trust them, but this oil really does work, even on horses. When my horses ache after a long day, they become very happy when they smell the oil that I bring to rub on them."

"Who are those people?" I asked, venturing that they might have been Gypsies.

"No," Alfred said. "It's usually one man or two with a horse and wagon. Gypsies travel as families or groups. They don't usually sell things."

"Have you seen Gypsies?" I asked.

"Mostly in Europe," said Alfred. "But I have seen them here. They will ask for work sometimes, or put on music shows, or just steal from people. For various reasons, they just keep moving."

"Good thing they move on," Alfred continued. "Because I would have to deal with them if they committed a crime and stayed around."

"Where do they come from?" I asked.

"Someone said they came up from Milwaukee," Alfred replied. "Others said they came from the French population on the Mississippi. The ones I met certainly came straight from Europe, based on the way they speak and act. They were common in Lippe when I was growing up."

"The Gypsies once told me how they cook a chicken," Alfred continued. "They kill it, pack it in mud whole and bake it over a fire. They don't remove feathers or clean it. When it's done, they peal the mud off, which takes off the feathers and skin, and eat it. The innards provide all the moisture. They get a good meal with very little effort."

"Will you try that?" I asked.

"Probably not, but I'll let you do one of my chickens as an experiment," Alfred laughed.

Alfred admitted that he typically enjoyed engaging strangers in conversation, even if they were Gypsies. "They have an interesting culture, beautiful clothes and nice music," he said. "But I don't see how they can survive. Personally, I don't like them. I don't respect people who don't like to settle down or work. Not good citizens. Can't build a country with people like that."

"Germans always measure people by how they work," I commented. "What about the other immigrants, like the English, French, Bohemians, Norwegians?" I teased Alfred.

"They are like us," he said.

"What about the Irish?" I asked.

"Some have just moved into Meeme Township west of here" Alfred said. "Most of them seem to be staying out East. They had a tough time with the famine and the British. They seem like good people."

"But there is always discrimination against new groups, isn't there?" I asked.

Alfred thought for a moment. "You know, when we came over, the people already in America said that the Germans were just a bunch of peasants, that they we would never make it in America. Now we Germans seem to have joined with our critics to say the same things about the Irish and other newcomers."

"You are correct," I replied. "Sometime in the future, the Irish, who would by that time have settled in, will join with the rest of the people already in America to condemn the next immigrant group. It's the way of things."

"You are probably right," Alfred said.

CHAPTER 23 – LEITNER

In the summer of 1859, Alfred and I were asked to help the neighbor, Rolf Leitner, to construct a large barn. The Leitners were especially good farmers, frugal and able to make good business decisions. Over the years, they would have cash reserves large enough to easily establish sons on their own farms in the community. On occasion, the Leitners would lend money to neighbors when banks couldn't lend, wouldn't lend or couldn't match the terms the Leitners offered.

"Get me a hundred strong men, not younger than 15 and not older than 65!" the barn crew boss demanded as the construction neared.

The carpenters and masons had been there days before getting ready for this moment. The beams were all laid out with peg holes, appropriate notches and cut angles. There were teams of horses, ropes and pulleys.

The toughest part was the actual raising of the timbers and then the roof. The sides would come later. Once the main beams started going up, they all had to be secured with pegs and notches. Then came the cross supports and boards.

"Those damned square nails!" I complained to myself, when I saw the wooden boxes full of them. "When are they going to invent round nails!"

The new Leitner barn was to be 100 feet long, the largest in the community at the time. One of the horizontal beams at the roof line was made from two trees spliced together to make it 100 feet long. The longest beam I remember seeing anywhere was 65 feet long.

The early German barns in the Centerville area had gable, straight-lined roofs. Gambrel roofs would come later. The design of the barns was due in part to functionality, cost of construction, type of building materials available, weather, whatever style was popular at the time, or the preference of the builder.

Initial barn designs were cultural more than anything, based on ideas from the old country. The very first immigrants had no other designs in America to choose from since there were no barns or local barn-builders before they came.

Outside barn boards were nailed on vertically. They often had small slits between them, either intended, or because when boards still had drying to do, they would still shrink. The slits allowed hay in the mow to breathe, that is, to allow air in to help finish curing and drying. But slits would also allow weather to get in, so most farmers covered the slits with battons.

Because I didn't like heights, I was assigned to help with lower sides and flooring. Some men were not at all fazed by working up high. Others, like myself, preferred to stay near the ground. Barn builders understood this. There was one young man bragged that he wasn't afraid of heights. After climbing to the top of the building, he froze, and had to be lowered back down, amid considerable laughter, with a harness and ropes.

Buildings that needed more protection from the elements or contained insulation in the walls, like houses and chicken coops, would have boards nailed on horizontally and overlapped. Some cultures preferred horizontal boards on barns, but not the Saxons.

There were no hay bales in those days. Hay was put up loose. Attached to the rafters at the ridge in the barn was a hay trolley or carrier with pulleys and ropes. One end of the barn had a large door into the loft. Hay was lifted from the wagon with large hay forks that looked like tongs, trolleyed into the barn, and dropped into the appropriate mow.

At the Leitner barn-building, Christina was part of the meal crew. Elsa did some of the heavier housework, like hauling water and wood. Since children also came with families, keeping young ones out of harm's way was important. Elsa was also assigned to the children.

Something of a tomboy, Elsa would have been willing and strong enough to be part of the barn crew, but they wouldn't let women do those things back then. She did complain about it to the crew boss, generating a hearty laugh among the crew.

I sought out the Leitner children, finding little Amanda, then about two years old. I knew that Amanda, my great-grandmother-to-be, would one day marry Ludwig Wagner, forming a strong bond between the families that would last for a hundred years.

I also sought out an older sister Clarissa, now ten years of age, born just before the Leitners departed from Europe. Elsa told me the story of her voyage to America, some of which I already knew. Baby Clarissa became ill on the ship and appeared likely to die. The captain, fearing a contagious disease, ordered the family to throw her overboard. After he walked away, the mother, Angela Leitner, feigned sorrow, but hid the baby in her skirts. She kept Clarissa out of sight and sound, not an easy task, for the remainder of the journey. Clarissa would live to be 83.

The Leitners arrived in Centerville in 1849. They had intended to land in Sheboygan. When Angela heard that there were Saxons in the Centerville area, she said, "This is far enough, let's get off." I always find it incredible how little things, like impulses and quick decisions, can completely change history. Had the Leitners gone on to Sheboygan or elsewhere, I either wouldn't be here today or would be a different person.

Whenever I look at a map, it has always amazed me how European immigrants managed to find roughly the same latitude, climate, and vegetation they had in the old country. They established ethnic communities in America, feeling more comfortable with those of their own kind.

The barn-raising started smoothly, considering the challenges with the size of the project. Raising a barn can be a dangerous business. One false move could mean injury or death. I was aware from my knowledge of local history that someone working on this job would die, not from the barn-raising, but from the weather. He was a neighbor to the Leitners.

It happened on the third day. A thunderstorm moved in during the early morning. A young man, moving a wagon of hay with a team of horses into a shed at his home, was struck by lightning. For some strange reason, the man tossed his boots toward someone on the ground just before the lightning hit, shouting that he wouldn't need them anymore. I warned the crew the day before about impending weather and told everyone to be careful. One of the crew shouted at me, "What do you know about the weather?"

After the death, the barn framework was quickly secured. The rest of the work was delayed until after the funeral. No one paid any attention to me during the funeral. Elsa, however, would ask me later why I was so concerned about this specific storm. I would lie that I had an abnormal fear of thunderstorms after a neighbor in my youth in Lippe had been killed by lightning.

A decade later the eldest Leitner son and heir to the farm lost his leg in an accident related to rain. He and his wife were on their way to church with a horse and buggy when it began to rain. His wife opened an umbrella which then startled the horses, causing them to break into a gallop. Leitner lost the reins. In his attempt to regain control of the horses, he caught his leg between the horses and the buggy, breaking it in several places. He was taken back to the house where the local doctor amputated his leg on the kitchen table. The descendants still possess the artificial leg.

CHAPTER 24 – HOUSEBARNS

The Wagner housebarn, completed in 1849, was a single-story log building with the house part on the east side, a threshing floor in the middle and the livestock and feed storage part on the west side. It was roughly 25 feet wide and 60 feet long. When the new livestock barn was built in the late 1850s, animals and feed were moved there. The former livestock part of the house barn was used for extra bedrooms and equipment storage.

A new frame house would be built in 1871. The housebarn would be removed with its logs, boards and beams recycled into other buildings in the 1880s.

Cobblestones in the cow yard were the only evidence of the former housebarn left when I was growing up. There was no mention of the structure in family lore in my time. I only found out about the housebarn when I received a 1931 Manitowoc Herald article that featured the family farm and briefly mentioned the structure.

The design of the Wagner housebarn, with a house and a barn separated by a threshing floor, was more typical of central and northern

Germany than the more intimate combination of house and barn utilized by the Saxons. Although Christina's first husband Meyer, a Saxon, would have started the building, the design of it indicated that Wagner was the one who would have finished it.

The Leitner housebarn, begun in 1849, was definitely Saxon. It was a large structure, 30 by 70 feet, having three stories and a partial basement. It was a timber frame, or "fachwerk" building with a living unit on the east, livestock unit on the west, a second floor or story with two bedrooms over the livestock, and a large third story for hay or other storage. At different times, the livestock part of the second story housed sheep, goats or chickens.

The Leitner housebarn had no doored closets, just open corner niches with hangar racks. The reason for this was that houses were assessed for taxation based on the number of enclosed rooms.

The Leitner housebarn also featured a root cellar under the dining area. These were built into most houses of the time to store fruits and vegetables over the winter. The Leitner cellar had an arched brick and mortar ceiling. It was dug out after the housebarn above it was built, so the arched ceiling was made with wooden forms.

In cases where the cellar was built before the house was constructed over it, the arch was accomplished by first creating a dirt mound, setting and mortaring the bricks over it, and then removing the mound of dirt from underneath. The bricks were positioned perfectly, like a Roman bridge, so as not to collapse.

The Leitner housebarn was constructed of white oak, green ash and pine wood. The insulation in the outer walls, called "nogging," consisted of vertical, hand-split, wooden staves, coated with seven inches of mud and straw. Inside walls of the living unit were plastered and then splattered with calcimine whitewash tinted blue using a paint brush to create the effect of wallpaper. A chimney in the center of the building was built of home-made mud bricks. Mortar was made from locally-produced limestone. A third housebarn in the neighborhood, on the east side of Saxon Road near the Sheboygan County line, was dismantled in the late 1800s.

Housebarns were rare in America. When the Leitner housebarn was restored in the late 20th century, there were only three of its kind remaining in Wisconsin and only about ten in the United States. There are still many in Europe.

The need to have something built quickly to live in during the first winter forced most German immigrants in Centerville to consider starting with temporary log houses and other simple log structures instead of frame structures. The abundance of timber allowed immigrants to plan for multiple, use-specific, frame structures in subsequent years, skipping the idea of an all-in-one structure like a housebarn.

I have seen homesteads, like the one on our farm, in later stages of development in the 1950s-60s. A typical homestead would start with the temporary house, then work toward a permanent house, adding along the way a collection of buildings that could include a well house, outhouse, woodshed, machine shed, tool shed or shop (usually part of a shed), larger barn, chicken coop or chicken barn, pig barn, granary, smokehouse, ice storage house, milk house, garage, sometimes a dog house, "cluck" house (to isolate broody hens who wanted to try to hatch unfertilized eggs), corn crib, and then one or more silos. A summer kitchen was also common, part of the main house or separated after newer additions to the main house. I have seen German homesteads with 15 to 20 structures.

Saxon frame houses were typically rectangular with a main entrance in the middle of a long side. The house would often be split with a stairway to the upper floor near the entrance and a stairway to a basement under it on the opposite side. There would be a wood stove for heat in each side of the house. You would see the two chimneys on those houses, usually located toward the center rather than on the ends. Cooking

was often done in the attached summer kitchen. Porches, other extended entrances, window dormers, and pillars were not typically Saxon or
German but added in America.

Chapter 25 – Labor

Large families were sources of cheap, abundant labor and future security. When families weren't large, they borrowed labor from relatives. Hired men and maids were also commonplace. Maids would take added responsibility for household chores when the wife gave birth. Hired men would take added responsibility for outside chores if the husband became injured, which too frequently happened. My father and the Kaiser neighbor of his generation both lost fingers in accidents. Another neighbor lost an arm. Leg and back injuries were common. The old German farmers I knew when I was growing up were often arthritic and bent over.

It was common practice that young, usually teenage nephews, nieces and cousins would spend summers on relatives' farms to help with the work. Not only would larger families share labor, but city cousins would also get to learn farming.

A ten-year-old Leitner cousin named Oscar Klemme was to spend not just a summer but several long periods at the Leitner farm. His father, the mason and carpenter who lived west of Hika, had a large family, but was often short of cash. He farmed out his children to reduce his own financial burden.

During the first week of Oscar's arrival, the Leitners were clearing trees along the edge of their farm. The perimeter fence led deep into the woods. When Oscar who was helping them decided to go home early in the afternoon, the men instructed him to follow the fence back to the homestead.

For some reason, Oscar went west instead of east. He walked into the evening, eventually finding a road he thought would get him back home. Oscar ended up walking toward St. Nazianz, taking him almost twenty miles away. After nightfall, he finally saw a light in the window of a farmhouse. Too shy to knock, he was taken in by the farm family after they saw him peeking through a window.

When the Leitners returned to the house in the evening, there was no Oscar. The men returned to the woods to look for him. They searched into the night. No Oscar. The Leitners were in a panic. They sent a few men on horseback to some of the neighbors. Still no Oscar. They had to tell the Klemmes that their son was missing. The families feared the worst, that maybe a wolf or bear could have killed Oscar. The next day Alfred and I were also involved in the search. We rode and walked around for two days.

Elsa insisted on riding with me on one of the days. She made some excuse about not wanting to work another horse, so insisted on riding behind me on my horse. I tried not to make too much of it in front of the other people in the search party but having Elsa's arms on my shoulders or around my waist much of that one day was pure joy!

The St. Nazianz family, Catholics recently arrived from Baden in southern Germany, at first had trouble understanding where Oscar was from. There was a considerable difference between Baden and Saxony in the German dialects spoken. It took a couple of days before one member of that community was located who had business near Centerville and could take Oscar with him. He eventually found the Leitner farm.

The St. Nazianz man was thanked profusely. He accepted some coffee and food, and feed and water for his horses, but graciously turned down any payment for his efforts. Oscar, scared by the experience, was only mildly reprimanded.

Chapter 26 – Winter

Winters seemed to be more severe back in the 1800s. It was certainly true that the lack of forecasting and a lesser ability to deal with the elements contributed to the difficulty in dealing with the winters.

In early February of 1860, after a wedding that Elsa and I attended near Manitowoc, it snowed for three days. I left Elsa at Nanette's home in the city, intending to collect her two days later. Elsa would be stranded there for a week, but safe. No one had any idea of the severity of the storm that was coming.

The snow was as high or higher than the Hessel log house where I was staying. A strong wind created an opening in front of the door, so I could easily get out. Typically, the opposite was true, because nature always seems to find a way to block one's door or driveway to increase the need to shovel more snow!

One of my housemates, the Hessel hired man named August Theilig, and I managed to crawl over the high snow drifts on a couple of wide boards to the Wagner farm. The snow drift in the Wagner yard was about

15 feet high. We could not see the house except for the chimney. Alfred had managed to dig out of the house but could not reach his new barn where his livestock were now housed. There was so much snow in the yard that we decided to tunnel under the snow to the barn. We used pieces of burning firewood to help melt our way through.

After the snow, it got extremely cold. Someone said that Lake Michigan froze all the way over to Michigan, a rare event.

About a week later we got news that two teenage sisters froze to death about 20 miles to the west. They had walked to a party about a quarter mile from their house. At the appropriate hour, they headed home. Two men offered to walk them home and even take them in a buggy. They declined, stating that their home was near. As they walked, the wind blew up snow, blinding them. They became disoriented and lost their way. The hosts assumed that the girls had arrived at home. Their parents assumed that the girls had decided to stay at the friend's house. In the morning, they were not seen. Their bodies were found off the road in a field.

Predicting the weather in the mid-1880s was difficult, especially in winter. One could look at the skies or sense changes in barometric pressure or humidity. Often the predictions were no more precise than grandfather feeling something coming in his bones or aching joints.

In the summer, it was somewhat easier to predict weather. The color of the skies, shapes of the clouds, humidity, wind direction, presence of whirlwinds or dust devils, and the restlessness of horses, birds or flies were all indicators of weather. Alfred and Elsa both tried to out-forecast each other, sometimes having fierce but friendly arguments. In my youth, I was never able to out-smart my father on the weather.

Chapter 27 – Census

1860 was a Census year. Having worked on a future Census, I decided to offer my services. Ten years before, the 1850 Census taker in the area, obviously not a German, had had considerable trouble spelling German names. It made my ancestry research more difficult, sometime hilarious, in trying to figure out who some of the people were, disguised by poor spelling. I have two Toepel branches in my family. In 1850, one was spelled Dopel and one Taple. I can't imagine what happened to the Polish names! The same spelling problems occurred with immigrants upon entry into America at the various ports. Names on passengers lists published later were likewise abused.

I was hired for the 1860 Census in part because I spoke good English and was deemed to have a good command of the paperwork involved. Forms were not sent out as they would be later. The Census in 1860 was still an interview at the residence. I was assigned to be a Census taker in the Polish area in Newton and the Norwegian area in Valders. It was assumed by 1860 that someone in each family spoke enough English to deal with the Census taker.

During my family research, I had noticed on the 1860 Census and 1870 Census that German immigrants were moving away from stating their specific kingdom of origin to just saying that they were German or Prussian. This occurred even though Germany was not yet formed, and Prussia did not cover all the German-speaking states or kingdoms, including Saxony at the time. I also noticed during my dozen years in Centerville in the 1850s and 1860s that immigrants from various German states were increasingly referring to themselves as just Germans.

I got Elsa to apply too. She spoke good enough English to get the job. Elsa had read many books in English and we often spoke in English with each other.

Elsa was assigned to the City of Manitowoc, a more diverse community of Bohemian, German, English and other nationalities. Elsa loved her temporary job. It expanded her horizons. She made some cash. Elsa got a chance to spend several nights at Nanette's house. She also met the man she would someday marry as a widower, although he was still happily married at the time.

The Wagners hired one of the Kaiser teenaged girls to cover for Elsa when she was away.

CHAPTER 28 – DISABILITY

Elsa mentioned a young cousin about six years old who had a severe cognitive intellectual disability, referred to as "retarded" at the time. "I have only seen her once," she said. "The family just keeps her at home, locked in a room. She eats with her hands, sleeps on a dirty mattress and poops on the floor. They give her toys and things to play with. They bring her out sometimes when no one else is around."

"Is there a place where they could put her, a kind of hospital?" I asked. "I heard that they have such places in France." Elsa had heard of the asylums.

"No," Elsa replied. "There is no such thing here. It's too bad, those people need special care. It's just that it takes so much time, patience and money. Many of them die not long after they are born. People who have mental or physical problems have a tough life. The cripples, those with physical but not mental problems, have it a bit easier. May God bless them all in heaven!"

"Did you ever walk around the cemetery?" Elsa asked. "Did you see the graves in the front where they bury the babies? There are more babies than adults buried there," she continued. "There are many reasons why they die. Sometimes it's just a bad pregnancy, a weak mother, a baby that has no chance, a poor diet, lack of a good doctor, an illness, or things we don't yet understand."

In the beginning, Saxon Cemetery buried its babies in the front. When the settlers first came, the adults were mostly young and hardy. The children who were born after arrival would die in greater numbers, hence Elsa's comment. Dying adults would catch up in numbers later. Behind the children's section in the cemetery, adults would be buried in rows as they died, one after the other. Family plots and family grave stones would come after 1900.

"There is a problem with my cousin's family," Elsa continued. "The parents were themselves cousins, maybe too closely related. The children are kind of strange."

"Were the parents first cousins?" I asked. "Second-cousin marriages are legal and usually not a problem."

"I don't know," Elsa said. "Alfred would know. He likes family histories. He keeps track of who is related and who isn't, just for fun. Do you really understand why closely-related people shouldn't marry?"

"I couldn't really explain it," I lied. "But they say that inherited weaknesses are exposed in those close marriages. You see it in animals too."

"Do these cousin marriages happen often?" I asked.

"No," Elsa said. "But many of us, like I said, were already related where we came from. I know of one case not so far from here," she added. "There was a first-cousin marriage near my home. They had two daughters. One was born normal and one wasn't. One day the normal one got a new dress for her fifteenth birthday. She was so happy that she ran across the road to show it to her friend who lived on the other side. She didn't look and got hit by a horse and buggy. She died. The family was left with the girl who was not normal."

I had trouble with the descriptions used at the time to describe people with disabilities. I didn't blame Elsa for her use of words. She was using the terminology of the time. Elsa was always trying to be as respectful as possible for every situation she encountered. I still heard the word cripple when I was growing up. My great-uncle was on an asylum board. We no longer use the words cripple or asylum in those contexts. Yet, I can't remember how many times I heard the terms "nut-house" or "loony-bin."

Elsa told me about one young girl buried in the cemetery in Hika, about 12 years old, who died of meningitis. "The family and the local officials wouldn't let anyone near the body, but the family wanted to show her anyway," she said. "They put a glass over the coffin and showed her through a large house window. People filed past the window on the porch outside."

"Still many people wouldn't come, just sent their regrets," Elsa continued. "The family had trouble finding anyone to bury the poor child. They stayed away from the church and the village for a whole month. The school she attended closed for a week. Fortunately, there were no other cases."

"How would she get it and no one else got it?" Elsa asked me. "She was in school every day before she got sick."

"Some people are carriers," I replied. "They carry the disease, but don't get sick. Some people are just vulnerable. Diseases may exist in the air or in the soil but seldom affect anyone."

Chapter 29 – Circus

I got word that a circus was coming to Sheboygan. It was unusual for the Wagners to go to Sheboygan, but Elsa had grown up in the county and liked to go to Sheboygan at times. The cities Manitowoc and Sheboygan were each about 12 miles from Centerville. Centerville was in Manitowoc County and the City of Manitowoc was the county seat. In my time, however, we had more connections to Sheboygan because my immediate ancestors, for some reason, tended to marry toward Sheboygan rather than toward Manitowoc.

I bought circus tickets for the Wagner family. Six of us, including Elsa and me, went for a Saturday afternoon show. The Wagners called it a "freak show," the common term at the time. We saw a few elephants and a lion. There was a very tall man, several very little people, Africans, Arabs, and Chinese in their native attire, and a woman with a real beard.

Elsa, as cosmopolitan as she might have been for her time, couldn't imagine what she was seeing. The Wagner children too were astounded. Little Ludwig asked Alfred if he could buy an elephant for the farm! "He could pull three plows!"

"I heard once that a lion got away and the police had to shoot it," Alfred said.

"That's what would probably happen," I replied. "Can you imagine having a lion show up on the farm?"

"I would feel bad for the lion," Elsa said. "This is not their place. I don't understand how they keep lions in a small cage all their lives and then expect them to be nice during the show!"

Elsa asked me if I knew anything about Africa. "It's called the 'dark continent,' isn't it?"

"It's not dark," I replied. "We just don't know much about it."

"Do they have cannibals?" she asked.

"I heard that," I said. "But I don't think they are common. As far as I know, all continents had cannibals back in history. I wouldn't make much of it. Africa is just not as developed as we are, but it will be some-day."

"I hope so," said Elsa. "I don't like what people say about Negroes. They are slaves in the South and treated like animals!"

Elsa mentioned a young man she knew from Sheboygan County who decided to join the circus. He couldn't find a farm or didn't get on with the family, Elsa wasn't sure, so he left when the circus came through.

"The family lived only a few miles from where we settled," Elsa added. "I wonder whatever happened to him?"

I would one day meet descendants of the family. What I couldn't mention to Elsa at the time was that the granddaughter of that man who joined the circus would become a famous Hollywood actress.

CHAPTER 30 – CLOSER

In the meantime, Elsa and I were getting closer and closer. I started to worry. Should I marry her and then leave? Should we have sex? Should I opt to stay in the past? Could I leave an offspring in the past?

I came on a mission to see my ancestors for several reasons, to slip in and then slip out without a significant trace. I understood that I would be forgotten when I left. However, I found that this mission was not as easy as I expected. "This is totally weird," I thought. "Should I have done this?" But it was too late.

In any case, I knew I was not going to stay in the past and I was going to break Elsa's heart when I left. Elsa had complicated my mission and my life. "She was not supposed to be here!" I complained to myself. "I did not come to the past to fall in love!" I suddenly realized that I was indeed the mysterious person I had heard about in the future who broke her heart.

There were many times when I wanted to tell Elsa everything, but couldn't. However, my conversations and emotions transmitted subtle messages to Elsa. She seemed to accept what she couldn't understand.

Elsa once said to me, "I don't know who you are, and I don't need to know. I find you fascinating and comforting. You don't know me either," she added. "I'm probably just as strange as you are. That's why I don't fit around here. Let's leave it at that." I was happy that Elsa said that.

Despite the workload, Elsa and I had quality time together. When the sun went down, most outdoor work came to an end. Elsa still had housework, child care, knitting and such. I would help where I could before I returned to the Hessels, washing dishes, repairing things, all done by lantern light.

The Wagners turned in early. With them and the kids in bed, we were still within earshot in the small house. In the winter, Elsa and I talked quietly and behaved properly into the night. Occasionally we would read a book or a newspaper together. She was always surprised that I had problems reading the old German script. "You are more English than German," she would joke.

During the longer summer days, it was different. We hugged and kissed whenever we were out of sight. We had a favorite stump to sit on behind the barn. When I once suggested another location under trees a bit farther away, she told me without telling me why, that we would never go there. I would soon figure out that the location was too close to where she found her dead brother.

One day, we were sitting on our stump when we started getting under each other's clothes. Fortunately, we pulled back just in time as one of the Wagner children came around the corner chasing a chipmunk he wasn't going to catch. He looked at us, smiled a little and ran away.

"What if he tells someone?" I asked.

"He won't understand," Elsa said. "But we need to be more careful."

"What if Christina or Alfred catch us being too close?"

"Alfred won't say anything, although we don't want to put him on the spot. Christina can sometimes be harsh."

"What would she do?" I asked.

"She might insist that you not come here anymore. She might insist that I leave, which would be a disaster for me. I can't go back home," Elsa cried.

I asked Elsa why she couldn't go back home.

She replied rather forcefully, "I can't talk about it now. It's too complicated. It's too hard. But I will tell you sometime. Please trust me on this."

In the end, Elsa would never tell me. Neither would I ever pursue the matter again. I would never meet her family either. I knew that Elsa's mother had died not long after they came to America. Elsa's brother fought with her father. There were rumors of drinking, abuse, even incest. Some things are better left unsaid.

One day Elsa asked me to share a personal secret and then she would tell me one of her own.

"What do you mean?" I asked.

"Something you wouldn't tell anyone else" she said.

Then she quickly said, "Maybe you don't have any. I shouldn't embarrass you."

"No, I'm not so moral as I pretend, if that's what you mean," I laughed.

"But you seem to be a better person than most of us in many ways" Elsa ventured, continuing to be perplexed about me.

Then Elsa said, "I will tell you one of mine, but please don't tell anyone." Elsa paused for moment.

"What?" I smiled.

"Okay," she said, "I like to walk naked in the woods." She blushed and said, "Please don't tell anyone!"

I smiled. "What is wrong with that?" I asked. "How many young men go skinny-dipping?"

"Many!" she replied. I had heard more than once that Elsa had done it with a few of the boys herself.

"Sweetie," I replied, "I'd like to share that walking experience with you sometime!"

CHAPTER 31 – WAR

There was more and more talk of an impending war between the North and South. The Democrats continued to make concessions to the South to avoid conflict and keep the country together. The Whigs were ineffective. There was a new party called the Republicans that had formed in Ripon, Wisconsin, or somewhere in Michigan, depending on the story. They were opposed to secession and slavery and seemed to be willing to take on the South. A humble fellow from Illinois was running for president.

When the war did start, the call to arms took some of Centerville's young men away. Farmers were given exemptions. Wisconsin farmers grew much of the wheat for the war effort. Miners in the southwestern part of the state provided much of the lead for ammunition. Wisconsin industry manufactured considerable armaments and war supplies.

People with enough money could buy their way out of the draft. One of the eligible Wagner neighbors neither served nor came up with the cash. He fled to work in a lumber camp in the Wisconsin north woods near Ashland out of reach of the draft. He came back after the war, but a younger brother who joined him would settle there. As the war dragged on, some farm folk felt guilty or patriotic and enlisted anyway. There were multiple drafts.

Many of the recent German immigrants like Alfred were uncomfortable with the war. They were not feeling like Americans yet, or felt that it was not their war. They were still trying to get over all that they had experienced in Europe.

There was a rumor that one German immigrant from Sheboygan Falls had joined the Confederacy. It turned out to be false, but it took years for his descendants to clear his name.

I quit my harnessing job to get a farm deferment, working half-time for the Leitners and half-time for their neighbor across the road, Elroy Johannes. Serving in the war, killing or being killed was certainly not part of my mission! A Johannes brother enlisted as a medic.

For me, it became more practical to move one mile north to live at one of the farms I was working for. I chose to stay with Johannes because one of the family had already enlisted, increasing the need for another farmhand. The Leitners were well-stocked with men.

Elsa was not happy about my move, but she understood the need to be attached to a farm for the exemption. She was no fan of the war either.

The move gave me some physical distance that helped to refute some of the talk about us. It also gave me some opportunity to prepare for my separation from Elsa that I knew must eventually happen.

Leaving was going to be incredibly difficult. Most of what I had come to find out on my mission I had already accomplished in the first six months of my stay. Elsa had put a wrench in my plans. I concluded that staying would have been virtually impossible as I had to fulfill my life in the future. I was developing an idea for Elsa, however, that I would share with her later. In the meantime, I decided to extend my mission through the end of the war.

Elsa asked me who I thought was going to win the war. The beginning of the war went badly for the North. It often looked as if the South might win and secede. I nonetheless said I would bet that the Union was going to survive, and that slavery was going to end.

"You seem to be so sure of yourself," Elsa stated forcefully. "And you are always right."

"Who are you anyway?" Elsa would stare at me without saying it.

CHAPTER 32 – FIRE

On one very cold winter day in 1861, with temperatures about ten below zero, there was a barn fire a few miles northeast of the Wagner farm. The farmer was unusual in that he had twenty milk cows. His barn also had a lower story called a basement. The stone foundation of the lower story supported the upper story, the hay mow. The cows and youngstock lived in the lower story. With an upper story, a barn ramp (or barn hill) was often needed for access with machinery, horses and hay. In a few short years, most barns in Centerville would have upper stories and barn ramps.

"What does he need so many cows for?" neighbors would often complain. "Some of us have just one milk cow and a team of oxen! Is he trying to get richer than anyone else?"

"Nothing has changed," I thought. While America offered people many opportunities to make money and get ahead, the power of jealousy often kept neighbors in check. It was the same when I was growing up.

The fire brigade sounded a warning bell in Hika. We could not hear the bell from the farm, but all the neighbors could see the smoke. A couple of horsemen raced around the greater neighborhood trying to get help for the fire fighters.

The fire brigade had only two pieces of equipment. One was a ladder and bucket wagon built in the village in 1850. The other was a hand pumper purchased a few years later.

By the time I arrived, the flames had engulfed the hay mow part of the barn.

Firemen were throwing buckets of water around the door of the animal entrance to the barn while they got the pumper wagon attached to a source of water. It was so cold that the water could quickly freeze around the edges of the buckets and subsequently in the hoses.

The only water available for a fire in most cases was from a farm well and from a cistern in the basement of the house. A farm pond near the buildings, when it existed, was useful. Although some wells already had hand pumps and pipes down into the well, the top of the well could sometimes be removed to allow a fire hose to be lowered into the well. A small amount of water could also be drawn from a water tank in the barn itself. Nonetheless, saving this barn and other buildings like it from a massive fire during this time period was usually futile.

Two small boys came with their father to the fire. "Richard, John," I heard their father shout. "Stay out of the way, over by the house." I noticed them moving from one corner of the house to the other, either to get away from the freezing wind or to get away from the heat that was blowing in their direction from the barn. The firemen had to occasionally throw water on the house roof because embers from the barn were landing on it.

The firefighters managed to get the milk cows out, but because of the extreme cold, the cows, not understanding the fire, were trying to get back into the barn. There was considerable chaos with the animals. The cows were finally corralled in a shed. The sheep and small calves were rescued. Heifers were still in the back of the barn. They could not be reached as the fire was moving down into the animal area.

"What about the bull?" someone shouted.

"Leave him in there!" was the answer. "He will just attack us!" I could soon hear the bull and heifers bellowing. They were lucky if they suffocated before they caught fire.

Cows exposed to smoke would often get pneumonia within a few days and sometimes die. If they didn't die, they would suffer from lung damage, be less productive and live shorter lives. A decision had to made as to whether any of the surviving cows had enough exposure to smoke and needed to be slaughtered. The farmer and most of the firefighters figured that the cows had little or no exposure to smoke and would be okay. One cow would die, but it may have been from trauma.

I saw at least twenty rats and mice fleeing the burning barn with several confused cats on their heels. A raccoon ran toward the house. The cause of the fire was determined to be a lantern that was temporarily left on one end of the barn.

The pumper wagon would become famous. In October of 1871, the fire brigade with the pumper would be called to the Peshtigo Fire in northeastern Wisconsin where over a thousand, possibly two thousand people would subsequently perish. As they were starting toward Peshtigo, they were quickly called back to fight the Chicago Fire which had started on the same day. The pumper would be loaded on a railroad car and sent to Chicago.

The pumper, ladder and bucket wagon, and fire bell would all later be housed in the Hall of Flame Fire Museum in Kenosha, Wisconsin. The museum was then moved to Phoenix, Arizona where I would one day see the Centerville equipment.

There were other tragedies involving cattle. The next summer, a farmer would lose ten cows and heifers when lightning hit a tree that they were standing under for shelter during a rainstorm. The farmer had a string of bad fortune leading up to the event. This loss was something that may have put him out of business. Neighbors who could afford it decided to each give him one cow. Some farmers contributed cash. In the end, not only did the farmer replace his cattle, but he gained an extra horse, two sheep and some cash.

There was no insurance policy or company in the mid-1800s. Your best insurance was prevention and the goodwill of your neighbors.

House fires did also occur but were usually not as destructive as barn fires or mill fires. For one, houses were seldom without a person in them no matter what time of day. The main sources of fire were related to the kitchen stove, pipes and chimney. People were working around the stove many hours of the day. Anything that started burning was dealt with quickly. Great diligence was taken to preserve the house given its importance to the family and the farm.

The only time there may be no one around the house or the farm would be during a church event like the Sunday morning service. This was also the time when thieves would take advantage. The Wagners lost several chickens and some tools during one church service. They decided to assign one person to stay at home. The maid or hired man sometimes filled that need, although these would often be given weekends off to be with their own families. Later when English church services were added, some would attend the German service and some the English. The Wagners in later years would sometimes hire a Catholic maid or hired a man who had a different church schedule.

One group of thieves in another township started a barn fire with a cruel deed. As they were robbing the toolshed, they noticed a can of kerosene. Some barn cats were around. The thieves decided for fun to pour the fuel on the cats and light three of them with some matches. The cats ran in panic. One ran into the barn, lighting the hay and burning down the barn. Fortunately, it was summer and the cattle were all outside.

CHAPTER 33 – NANETTE

"What if you got pregnant and weren't married?" I asked Elsa hypothetically.

"I would have to get married in a hurry," she replied.

"What if you didn't want to marry?"

"How would I support myself?" Elsa replied. "I would be ostracized for sure. No one would marry me later. I would be defiled, like my friend Nanette."

"There are always exceptions," I said. "Every generation has those issues. There are men who will love women despite their past just like there are women who will love men despite their past."

"You don't understand," Elsa said. "It is harder for women."

"But doesn't Nanette have an exceptionally difficult family?" I asked. "Not everyone needs to be ostracized."

Elsa then told me the story about her friend. Nanette, who was Bohemian-German, was born in Newton but now lived in Manitowoc. Although I had met her, I had only pieces of the story. Nanette was in her mid-teens when she got pregnant. Her parents were livid. Even if they weren't so angry as they acted, as parents they were expected to uphold the family name and their religious values. "I will shoot the son of a bitch if I ever see him!" the father once shouted.

Everyone in Nanette's community seemed to know who the boyfriend was or thought they did. Nanette's parents did not seem to know. Nanette refused to name anyone, which led to the false idea that there may have been more than one relationship.

Nanette moved to a relative's house in Manitowoc, had the baby and put it up for adoption.

"Nanette, who is now a seamstress, comes to see me sometimes but avoids most of her neighbors," said Elsa. "I worry about her a lot. She is so thin, never looks well. I figured she would eventually get over the baby and her parents, but it weighs on her."

"The whole issue made me wonder about the cost of this kind of shame versus the societal value of stable families and relationships," I commented. "Whatever the circumstances, shouldn't all children be a blessing? Life is too short."

We decided to visit Nanette one Sunday. She showed us around the city. I was surprised that Nanette, who spoke both German and Bohemian, preferred to converse in English with Elsa. It was as if Nanette was trying to remove her parents from her memory.

CHAPTER 34 – TEACHER

"Why didn't you become a teacher?" Elsa asked me one day. "Your family was well educated from what you told me about them, and you are obviously educated. Besides, you seem to be wise beyond your years."

"Thanks, but I have no particular desire," I replied. "I don't think I would have enough patience to deal with a schoolhouse full of children of eight different age groups."

"Why don't you become a teacher?" I then asked Elsa.

"Few women are even allowed to become teachers," she replied. "I would have to stay single. I would have to attend a normal school for training which I can't afford."

"Wouldn't Alfred help you?" I asked.

"He would, but he hasn't much money. We've been living in that primitive house for over a dozen years. Many of the neighbors are building new houses. I know it bothers him. He isn't the best businessman around. He works hard but talks about things he never gets around to doing."

All local schools in Centerville at the time were one-room schools, usually with about thirty students but sometimes several more or several less. There would be only one teacher and he would be required to teach all subjects.

"Could you help me to become a teacher?" Elsa asked. "I finished grade school. I read a lot in both German and English."

I thought about it for a moment and then said, "I've been wanting to support you somehow. I have some money saved up."

"But you need your money to get a place of your own," she replied, not really wanting to suggest that idea. I didn't answer, just smiled. I knew I would not be needing a permanent place of my own.

Most of the grade schools at the time were taught in the local immigrant language with English as a subject. In Centerville, most subjects were taught in German. However, schools were slowly moving toward English, in part because newer textbooks were only available in English. Elsa could certainly handle both languages.

However, there was still considerable resistance to moving entirely to English. I knew that when a future Governor of Wisconsin in the latter part of the century proposed a law that all public and private schools must teach its basic courses using English, he was voted out of office after only one term.

Elsa never would become a teacher but continued to read books voraciously. She even read Kant, and "God forbid," I thought, "Elsa somehow managed to find a book about Darwin and evolution." When Christina found the book and realized what it was, she burned it, but did not raise her voice about it. The Wagners knew that Elsa was going to be Elsa. They always knew that she was going to rebel at times yet was a very special person.

I felt that way also. It was Elsa who enabled me to open up about culture, religion, women's issues, war, immigration and other topics of the day.

Elsa would have a positive influence on the Wagner children. Ludwig would someday be honored by the University for his outstanding farming and community service. Otto would become a teacher, editor, businessman and serve over thirty years as a county clerk. Melanie would marry a successful farmer and community leader and raise a large well-educated family, including two sons who would become engineers.

CHAPTER 35 – VISION

Alfred was invited one evening to a friend's house for a birthday party. Arthur Klein had turned fifty and invited a small number of his male friends. The party occurred in the dead of winter. His house was about four miles from the Wagners. Alfred invited me to come along. We took a horse and buggy. When we arrived, Arthur helped to unhitch the buggy and put the horse in the barn. He did this for all of his friends.

After a few hours of food and drink, the guests began to leave. Arthur's close neighbor and best friend offered to help him with the horses, but Arthur insisted on doing the first one himself. He went out and was gone for some time. One of the other men went out, finding Arthur lying on the floor in the barn. He helped him back into the house, thinking that Arthur had had too many drinks.

"Not so," said Arthur. "I'm not drunk!"

He then proceeded to explain that he had seen a vision. In the vision, there was a funeral. He did not know who had died. The coffin was closed. Arthur and most of his friends were pallbearers. He pointed to his friends in the room. "You were a pallbearer, you, you, you, you and you, pointing lastly at Alfred." Only his best friend was not a pallbearer and not in the vision. The men then laughed and said, "Nonsense, you had too much to drink!"

The next morning, word came that Arthur's best friend had died of a heart attack at the breakfast table. The men in the vision would become the pallbearers. We were stunned when we heard about it. The story was published many years later by Arthur's daughter, a marriage relative whom I remember meeting at our farm when I was young. I had forgotten the incident.

"What does this all mean?" Elsa asked.

"It means that there are things about the future that may be predicted or pre-determined," I ventured.

Chapter 36 – Runaway

In the summer of 1862, Alfred and I were getting ready to make hay one morning at the Kaisers when Junior came running to tell us to come home immediately. One of the neighbors had found a Negro sleeping in his barn! "They brought him over to our place because you are the guy with the badge!" Junior said, quoting the neighbor. "It looks like somebody beat him too!" he added.

Two of the Kaiser men, Alfred and I ran back to the Wagner farm. The black man was sitting on a chair by the door of the house. He appeared to have an injured arm. Christina had offered him some coffee and food plus whiskey for his wound. The smaller children were peering from behind the door post.

Elsa was talking to him. She quickly looked to me.

"He is a runaway slave. What should we do?"

"I should call the sheriff," Alfred replied automatically.

"We can't send him back!" Elsa pleaded. "We need to help him get to Canada!"

"I agree with Elsa," I said. "The South will send vigilantes to pick him up. And who knows what will happen to him if he goes back."

"Wisconsin has not honored the Fugitive Slave Act," I added. "Legally he could probably stay, but realistically he is in danger of being returned. There are people in the North who would just as soon return him for reward money. There are people who might even threaten his life!" We had heard that one escaped slave was lynched by a hostile mob somewhere in southern Wisconsin while another was rescued from jail by a friendly mob.

In the meantime, Elsa was trying to find out more about the man. She had trouble understanding his English.

"Let me try," I said.

His name was Jeremiah Jackson. He came from Missouri. His wife, whom he called "Fancy," had just died. The four children were then sold off. Jeremiah looked to be about fifty. He was tired, had not eaten well, but otherwise looked fit. Jeremiah had been attacked by dogs, but his arm injury did not appear to be serious. He had spent a night at a church in Elkhart Lake and then headed for Centerville, looking for another church in the area. He was trying hard to avoid cities, sheriffs and mobs.

Alfred said that the Lutheran Church could possibly help, but that he knew that the Catholic Church had been part of the "Underground Railroad" as they called it. It was rumored in the past that a priest in northern Manitowoc County kept a secret room in his parsonage where he had stowed runaways before.

Deciding to ignore his official obligation to contact the sheriff first and his religious obligation to contact the Lutherans, Alfred decided that he would go directly to the Catholic Church in Hika. He would accept whatever consequences that may occur with his chain of command later.

In the meantime, Alfred, using me as an interpreter when he couldn't understand, asked more about Jeremiah's background. Did he have a weapon? No. Had he committed any crimes? No. Could he read and write? About second grade level.

The Wagners had not seen an African American before, whom they called a "Negro," since passing through New York. They had never spoken to one before.

Jeremiah was finding it difficult to relax. One could tell that he didn't really trust anyone. Despite the Wagner hospitality, he knew that time was always against him.

Having a black man at their house was both novel and awkward for the Wagners. They knew that word would get around and curious neighbors would come to see the man. The sheriff would eventually hear about it. We assured him that people on Saxon Road would not harm him.

The Catholics accepted responsibility for Jeremiah and arranged to send him north. Not wanting to have him seen in the village while they arranged transport, they asked that Jeremiah spend a night at the Wagners. They would send a buggy before daylight. Jeremiah would have to be hidden to escape detection.

It was quite an evening! I stayed late while Alfred, Elsa and I listened to an incredible story about the inside of slavery. Jeremiah said that while some slaveholders were good Christians, they were still slaveholders. A few of his white neighbors did not keep slaves at all and were sometimes ridiculed for that. Jeremiah's owner was cruel. It was time to run, he said, after his children were gone. Jeremiah did not have any hope that the South would give up slavery, even if they lost the war with the North. He hoped to be reunited with his children someday.

Elsa gave Jeremiah her address, asking him to write when he was safely in Canada. Some months later, Elsa got a letter from a sponsor family in Canada stating that Jeremiah was safe. "He expresses his heartfelt thanks!" the sponsor stated.

Alfred was later criticized by the sheriff, as expected, for circumventing his authority. Jeremiah had already been moved out of his jurisdiction before the sheriff got the news.

Nonetheless, the sheriff was sympathetic. "I guess I would have done the same thing," he smiled. Plus, he plainly didn't want to deal with the issue. The sheriff decided not to communicate the matter with any other neighboring authorities.

Alfred and the sheriff then got into a long conversation about the progress of the Civil War. As much as Wagner believed in the preservation of the Union and the abolishment of slavery, he was no fan of the war. "We left Europe to get away from war," he repeated several times.

CHAPTER 37 – SCARE

As if there was nothing else to worry about in 1862, a neighbor arrived on horseback at the Wagner farm early one morning to warn us that local Indians were planning to attack the white settlers to drive them out of the region. He suggested that people might be safer in the village. After hearing the man out and consulting with the family, Alfred decided to sit tight and defend the property. I got the news at the Johannes' and rode immediately to the Wagners.

I strongly urged the Wagners not to panic. I knew from my history that this was a false rumor but couldn't divulge it. I mentioned that there had been Indian scares before and nothing ever came of them. Besides, the Indians had been subdued and greatly weakened in most of the state. Elsa backed me on this.

Nonetheless, to be safe, the Wagners armed themselves and stood ready. Elsa was given the family rifle. Alfred brandished his pistol. I ran over to the Kaisers, who always had plenty of guns, to borrow two of their firearms. Alfred was no longer Justice of the Peace by this time and left decisions about the township to other authorities.

Elsa and I sat up most of the night on our favorite stump to stand guard. It was one of those times when we talked so much about everything that we felt we had solved all the problems of the world. Except ours, of course! Toward morning we fell asleep huddled together next to the stump.

Several Centerville residents panicked and fled to the village. They gathered in Hika, fleeing onto the piers with their families and weapons. Fearing that the Indians might destroy the entrances to the piers and trap the residents, it was then decided to evacuate those who wanted to leave either to Sheboygan or Manitowoc. The next morning after hearing no other news, I took a horse to Hika to see what was going on.

Nothing came of it. This was the second Indian scare in the area, but again no Indians. Later we heard that the recent scare was apparently started by Southern sympathizers attempting to interfere with a Union effort to draft more soldiers. A second rumor was that the scare started with some loose talk in a bar about forty miles away. A contributing factor were the Indian Wars of 1862 in Minnesota and the Dakotas that kept immigrants in the Midwest on edge.

Gennie Sunshine, a half Indian herself and in a better position to know what Indians were thinking, was livid about the Indian scare, stating again and again that the remaining Indians would not be able to uproot the white settlers.

"When there are no sources of information other than a weekly newspaper, an occasional telegraph or man on horseback, the rumor mill is an incredibly powerful tool in shaping opinion," I told Elsa when we reminisced about the Scare. "It could also be said that when one deliberately limits oneself to only one or two sources of information, the effect of those sources becomes greatly magnified, and the effect of a single rumor also becomes greatly magnified."

"What other sources are there?" Elsa asked.

Not able to mention future media, I said, "You just need to read more to be able to balance your opinion. People who are old and wise or have extensive experience or travel are also good sources of information."

Chapter 38 – Illness

One day Elsa complained about feeling nausea. She did not seem to have a fever. "You may have a touch of influenza," I told her.

The nausea continued for another three days. Elsa did not vomit but felt weak and didn't want to eat. Then her skin turned yellowish. She mentioned that her urine was dark-colored.

"You have jaundice, a liver problem," I said.

"Is it serious?" Elsa asked.

"We should call the doctor. It might be something like hepatitis," I ventured.

"How do you know?" Elsa asked. "I had it when I was young," I replied. "Hopefully it's nothing more serious."

The doctor arrived with a flurry of questions. Elsa had no drinking problem, of course, that would affect her liver, and no previous symptoms. Until a few days ago, she was able to digest foods with fat or oil.

"Have you eaten any uncooked or other unusual food in the past month?" the doctor asked. "Any contaminated water?"

Elsa mentioned that she had food at a church social in Newton about a month ago.

"I also attended," I added. "The food seemed to be okay."

"Like your friend here," the doctor said pointing at me, "I think it's hepatitis. But call me in a few days if it gets worse. Some people can carry hepatitis and don't get sick. Most people are immune if they had it when they were young. If it's hepatitis, you will get over it, but it will take time. It seems to hit adults harder. If it's something worse, you will also need to pray," the doctor added carefully.

"With hepatitis you cannot digest fatty foods and your liver cannot store sugar" the doctor continued. "You will feel weak between meals. You need to eat eggs and lean meat. You can eat bread and vegetables, but a little at a time and frequently. Stay away from fat and sugar. There is no medicine for this. The main thing is to rest. Stay in bed more or sit in the sun or by a warm fire. It may take month or more."

"No lard for you any time soon!" I joked to Elsa.

"Hepatitis is contagious, so do not touch other people for at least ten days," the doctor continued. "Bathe often, wash your clothes and bedding. We do not want others in the house to become sick. I will come back the day after tomorrow to see how you are doing. In the meantime, I will contact the church in Newton to see if anyone else got sick."

Elsa was weak and depressed. I hated seeing her like this. I suddenly realized that she was mortal and that I could lose her here.

But her skin color and urine soon returned to normal. "You will get over it," I assured her.

Elsa gradually improved but lost weight and was not feeling normal for about two months. She was disappointed that she was not able to eat fatty foods, especially the lard sandwiches that she liked to eat in the cold weather. I never saw her eat lard again after that.

I sat with Elsa whenever I could. I found her more books to read. Sometimes I read to her. We talked in English a lot. The English bothered Christina because she never learned it well, but the children picked it up readily, repeating things we said.

Elsa's illness made us think about each other more. She dropped her guard somewhat and some of her inhibitions, hugging me in front of the Wagners, asking me to assist her to walk to the toilet, asking me to bring her blankets and sets of clothes. If we weren't like family before, we were now. I still had to go to work at the neighbors but found myself aching and distracted. Both the Johannes and the Leitners would give me half-days off or told me now and then to sleep at the Wagners. I still got my full salary which I promised to make with extra time later.

Elsa's illness forced the Wagners to put off some projects. Alfred had to spend more time around the house. The children were able to pick up some of the slack. Fortunately, Elsa's illness occurred in the early winter when there was less work outdoors.

"I didn't realize how much work Elsa did around here," Alfred admitted.

Eggs were a little hard to find this time of year because chickens typically take time off from laying during the reduced daylight in the fall to molt, changing out their feathers and using much of the protein in their diet for that purpose. I begged some extra eggs from the neighbors. I then suggested to the Wagners that they add some lantern light for an hour or two each day and give some extra grain to the chickens to stimulate egg production. Egg production increased immediately.

"How did you know that?" Elsa asked.

CHAPTER 39 – TREE

Ludwig Kessler had come on the boat from Germany with the Meyers, Freiburgs and Hessels. He was a Saxon, but from another part of the kingdom. They met on the way to Bremen and decided to come to Wisconsin together. The Kesslers became good friends of the Meyers, Hessels and Freiburgs. After Christina's husband Friedrich died, Ludwig would sometimes visit Christina to console her and offer a hand with the farm.

Ludwig's family had a history of military service. Although he never served himself, he had an air of discipline about him that reflected his upbringing. Ludwig's farm was about three miles northwest of the Wagners. He established a beautiful homestead, small but modern and ahead of its time.

I once asked Ludwig when he was having coffee at the Wagners how Saxony became Protestant. "Luther started the Reformation in Wittenberg on the northern edge of Saxony," he replied, "near where I came from." Christina added that the Lutheran church in her hometown had been established by the Catholics before the Reformation arrived in her hometown. "It was a typical Catholic structure," she said. "It was just like the older church in a nearby town, built on the highest hill in the area with a tall steeple."

When the Civil War started, Ludwig's son volunteered to serve. There were no other children. Ludwig in his usual disciplinarian way tried to do his work by himself, including clearing more trees.

One day he cut a tree that fell the wrong way, landing on his wagon. As he tried to get the horses out of harm's way, he was trapped between the wagon and the tree. Ludwig was able to cut one of the horses free of its harness. The horse then ran home but was not noticed by Ludwig's wife for more than an hour. Meanwhile, the tree began to shift, eventually suffocating Ludwig.

Although the usual obituary read that he did not suffer much, the neighbors figured he was pinned for some time, trapped and struggling to escape and breathe. One neighbor, who thought that he heard someone yelling but dismissed it, was devastated.

Ludwig's son was called back from the war. He had been injured on the front lines and was assigned to a support role. He was unable to run the farm, leaving after the war for the West. Ludwig's widow sold the farm, now only a shadow of its previous glory, to a Leitner.

Chapter 40 – Lincoln

As the war drew to a close, I couldn't sleep, knowing that Lincoln would be assassinated. "I could prevent it!" I thought to myself but was not able nor willing to do it. Well, I could try. If I sent a message somehow, probably no one would believe me anyway. If I travelled to Washington and physically put myself in the scene between Booth and Lincoln, I could save the President. Or if I failed to stop it or get anyone's attention, I could then become part of the conspiracy and perhaps charged.

Caesar heard warnings from his wife and the soothsayer and still went to the senate. "God will have His will in the end," I thought, even though I didn't believe Lincoln's death had anything to do with God. Saving Lincoln, most historians would agree, would have made the post-war much easier.

Elsa saw how stressed I was in April of 1865. I literally paced the floor in front of her. She had no idea what was up.

"Are you planning to leave me?" she fretted. I said nothing.

When word came that Lincoln had died, she saw my reaction.

"Can you see the future?" she asked. "Who are you?" she said again much louder than before.

I could not give her a straight answer. "Some people, as you know, have this burden of feeling things," I shouted. "I can't explain them and don't know if they can trust their instincts! I feel many things, have nightmares sometimes, yet most of them don't happen and they don't make any sense." I assured her that the future was out of my hands, even if I guessed correctly at times. "God is in charge, not me!"

"But you saw that Lincoln was going to die, didn't you? You could have done something about it!"

CHAPTER 41 – TYPHOID

"Gennie Sunshine died last night," Elsa told me one morning in the summer of 1865.

The first rumor, that it was a murder, turned out to be false, like a lot of rumors about Gennie. Gennie had died of typhoid. Alfred, no longer Justice of The Peace, but acting for the current one who was ill, was called to the scene to find out what happened. The doctor ordered that Gennie's bedding and clothes be burned. The children were ordered to bathe and avoid contact with the public for two weeks. Someone recommended the house be cleaned with borax, a chemical that was known but not commonly available at the time. Lye was used instead. Food was brought to the house. Alfred bathed carefully when he got home and slept in the barn for a few nights.

"Gennie deserved what she got," some said about her demise.

Elsa was angry. "Gennie was not the best person, but she had a tough road to follow, given her background and not being married. May God be kind in His judgment!"

Most in the village defended Gennie's honor. She was nonetheless buried alone in a far corner of the cemetery, obviously shunned in death.

The children were farmed out to relatives or accepting families in the neighborhood as was the practice of the time. There were no foster homes in those times. My grandmother's family raised two children from a family of fourteen when both parents suddenly died.

Chapter 42 – Mourning

Nanette's father Ernst got cancer. Nanette went home to see him. It was not easy. He was still bitter and so was she. Only Nanette's mother was now forgiving. Ernst was only 55. The family had left their original church and joined another church toward Kiel to the west. It was a sadder than the usual funeral, as funerals go. The body was not shown. Nonetheless, Nanette got to see several relatives and former neighbors she had not seen for years.

Nanette visited Elsa and me at the Wagner farm for a couple of hours after the funeral. She was thin and looked as if she had aged another five years from the previous time that I had seen her. I wanted to tell Nanette but couldn't that children born to young women out of wedlock would be less controversial in the future. We consoled her as much as we could, hoping that her father's passing would remove a burden from her. It would not.

After Nanette left, I decided to ask Elsa what she knew about the pregnancy. "I didn't know her at the time, Elsa replied, because I was still living at home."

"Why do you ask?"

"Just wondering," I replied.

"Do you think that someday women will have more respect than we have now?" Elsa asked. "I mean, if they get pregnant too young like Nanette, why do they bear the brunt of the blame? It's bad enough to go through the pregnancy and the pain, but then be forced to give up the baby to adoption, then have one's reputation ruined, then realistically not be able to marry, and then, as a woman, not able to realistically support oneself. It isn't fair!"

"I suffer too," Elsa continued. "Just because I haven't found a husband, evil people think that Nanette and I are having sex! I love Nanette as a friend, not as a lover! I'm tough, I can take it, but Nanette is sensitive. She needs emotional support. Nanette is a very good person who made a mistake. She gets little sympathy. People criticize her to her face, even more than ten years after the event. They call her bad things behind her back. Christians are supposed to forgive, aren't they?"

"What about her partner?" I asked. "How old was he? Wasn't he taking advantage of the situation? He should at least take his share of the blame!"

"You are right!" Elsa said. "I think he was 18, also immature, but other than being threatened by the family, not taking much blame or responsibility. He could have married her!"

Elsa continued to vent. "This story about Eve causing original sin, it's just a bunch of crap. By the way, when are women going to be able to vote? When are they going to be able to run for political office? When are they going to be able to serve in the ministry or even vote in their churches?"

Elsa finally gasped a sigh of relief after so much frustration. She had tears in her eyes.

I grabbed Elsa and hugged her. "It will get better," I assured her. "But it will take time. Let's spend more time with Nanette." I knew but couldn't tell Elsa that Nanette would eventually die in Elsa's lifetime.

Chapter 43 – Bull

A man was killed on a Sunday afternoon by a dairy bull. As was the custom, people would either entertain at home or go out to visit on Sunday afternoons. Charlie Kramer and his wife Lola were getting ready to go out. Charlie had the horse hitched to the buggy. Lola was late in getting ready, so Charlie decided to go out in the barn to check on the animals, pushing the hay up to the cows, scraping the manure that was under the cows into the gutter, and checking on anything else that needed attention. He did this every time he was in or near the barn, often four or more times each day. All farmers routinely went out to the barn to check on things, especially just before they went to bed.

Bulls were usually kept for two years or less, so they would not get a chance to breed their heifer daughters coming into the herd. Charlie and his current bull, named Buchanan after the former President, were friends, so he thought. The bull was kept in a pen in the far corner of the barn. The hay feeder was attached to the back wall of the pen, so in order to give the bull more hay, Charlie had to open the gate, walk past the bull and fork hay into the feeder. He did this every day and the bull was always happy to get fed.

On this particular day, the bull attacked Charlie, chased him around the barn, and pinned him against a post, killing him. There was much speculation as to why the bull turned on the man. "Bulls can be flighty and attack for no reason," some said.

Elsa knew the couple. We attended the funeral. We found out that Charlie had shaved just before going to the barn and probably had an odor of shaving cream on him. It is quite possible that the bull did not recognize Charlie because of the strange odor.

After the funeral, Elsa said to me, "It goes to show what can happen when a woman can't get dressed on time!"

The bull was shot and hauled to the butcher. Lola sold the farm in the spring and moved into town.

Chapter 44 – Auction

Farm auctions were rare in the 1860s. Usually there was a son willing to take over the farm. Or the farm might be sold intact. Most farmers owned so little personal property that an auctioneer wouldn't be necessary. Farmers in financial trouble would often be bailed out by their neighbors.

However, there was one such auction in the Wagner neighborhood. The farmer and his family decided to join a brother's business in town. Like Alfred, the owner had not been a farmer in the old country. He had trouble getting used to the rigors of farming. He dreamed of a less-demanding city life.

Alfred asked Junior to stay home from school to attend the auction, but Junior was so shocked that a close neighbor might really sell out and move, that he preferred to be in school that day. That neighbor's son was also Junior's best school friend. Junior, like most young boys, didn't like school very much. However, on this day, almost in tears, he ran off to school early.

Alfred and I attended the auction. Alfred was looking for another milk cow. He tried to buy a Jersey from that neighbor before the auction but was told that all the cows had already been consigned. As trees fell and more acres were available for agriculture, there was increasing demand for livestock and farm equipment. The farmer decided he might do better with an auctioneer.

I was very curious to see what the sale prices would be. I had gotten used to the costs of things in the mid-1800s, but still was surprised by the high or low values of items compared to those in my present life. The price of a normal milk cow in my time in Manitowoc County would likely not exceed the price of an acre of land, but in the 1860s land was still under $10 per acre.

Alfred was hoping to get the cow for twelve dollars, but bidding went up to eighteen. He bought her anyway. When Christina heard about the price, she was angry. "We don't have such money," she murmured. "Why didn't you buy a Friesian? They are bigger cows, give more milk and have more meat!"

The little Jersey turned out to be a good investment in the end because she delivered seven out of eight heifer calves before she got too old to conceive. Jerseys also have a higher content of fat and protein in the milk, more important for butter and cheese. The little Jersey was the cow that I would often have to milk when I was around the farm.

By the end of the century, the Wagners would get into the registered Jersey business. We still had Jerseys when I grew up in my time. After I left farming and became a professor, I once stopped to admire a large herd of Jerseys in a field along a highway. As I stood next to my car, forty Jersey cows made their way to the fence to greet me. It was one of my favorite Jersey moments!

Alfred loved this cow so much that he would never sell her even when she no longer produced calves or milk. After Alfred died, Christina intended to slaughter the cow, but the children objected. The cow, named "Number 21" because it was Alfred's good luck number, died a natural

death on the first anniversary of Alfred's death. She was buried behind
the barn near our stump.

CHAPTER 45 – GENERATIONS

I asked Alfred one day about the next generation on the farm. Would he want his children to farm or do something else?

"Traditionally, the oldest son has first choice to buy the farm," Alfred replied. "The one who gets the farm must also pay shares to his siblings. Sometimes the older sons are wanting farms before the father is ready to retire, so they look for other properties. The daughters typically go with their husbands."

"Junior has first choice," Alfred continued. "He seems really interested in farming. I have three other sons, so I'm not worried about someone taking over. But it's their choice as to what they want to do. Just about every family these days has a cheesemaker. Just about every family has a businessman in town. With land opening in the northern part of the state, some of our children will move north." I knew that several Centerville children would move to Clark, Marathon and Lincoln Counties in northern Wisconsin.

"I have seen too many families lose a child along the way," I reminded Alfred.

Alfred was taken aback for a moment. "I don't want to be pessimistic," he said. "But you are right. We have big families for love of children and for labor, of course. We never expect to lose children. But I have already lost one. Christina has lost two."

"What I am concerned about at this point is my retirement," Alfred continued. "The Germans have a 'bond of maintenance' tradition where the next generation takes care of the older generation. We could live together in the same house. Often, we build a new second one for either the older generation or the younger generation. The bond is usually a written contract that would also include provision of food, heat, garden space, maybe even a cow for the older generation. The guarantees continue as long as the older generation lives."

"Realistically, the bond depends, of course, on whether we get old enough to retire," Alfred joked. "It depends on how well we get along with the son taking over. Sometimes the old man is just too crusty to have around the house," he laughed. "Sometimes the old lady and the daughter-in-law can't work together in the same house. Farmers never really retire, you know, we just work until we drop or fade away."

The bond of maintenance was the elderly health care and housing system until modern times. Even when I was growing up, I often saw three generations living in one house. Most houses had at least four or more bedrooms. The Wagners would have six in their next timber-frame house. I knew of one house in the neighborhood that had eight bedrooms.

Multi-generational houses had a good distribution of labor, more efficient use of heat, food, clothing and other resources, better discipline, a variety of ideas, more physical and emotional security, and more wisdom under one roof. Hired men and maids would also be there.

Even the public grade-school teachers were housed by members of the school board. The Wagners, Kaisers and Leitner's all served on the local school board and all housed a teacher at one point or another.

Multi-generational houses were a rich experience.

I asked Alfred if he thought that men or women would live longer. "Men are stronger," he said. "But women seem to live longer. I never thought about that," he pondered.

I mentioned that women have the extra challenge of childbirth that could often shorten their lives. Men take more risks and too often don't take good care of themselves because when they are young, they think they are invincible. I couldn't mention the disadvantage that the Y-chromosome gave to men because it was not known at the time.

"I think nature just wants men and other males out of the way earlier because they tend to block the progress of the next generation," I joked. "Old females blend in better, old males just get in the way."

CHAPTER 46 – JUNIOR

Alfred and I continued our conversations. He did not try to figure me out, just accepted what he saw. Alfred talked about buying another 40 acres to the north that he thought might come up for sale. I knew that this would happen, but after his death. In fact, the Hessel farm across the road would also be owned by two Wagner generations. Alfred hoped that his sons would get into farming. He wanted his oldest son Junior to have the farm if he wanted, as was the custom.

Sadly, Junior would not live to get the farm. Only a teenager, he wanted to be of use everywhere on the farm. Junior learned how to handle an axe and other wood tools. He began helping to clear the land. Alfred and I watched him carefully so that he would not hurt himself. Junior seemed to be too anxious at times to get things done.

The farm had been cleared to the west as far as a small creek, leaving about a third of the farm still wooded. Clearing 50 some acres in a little over a dozen years was no small feat when employing only a few people at a time, I realized. The back part of the farm was hilly and steep.

Alfred was content to slow down with the clearing for the moment while he planned to build a new frame house in the next few years. I knew what was going to happen. Just as the new house was being finished, Alfred would suddenly die. It was ironic that Friedrich Meyer never lived in the new house that he started building, and that Alfred never lived in the new house that he was building.

One day, Alfred had some business in the village. Since I was still working for Leitner and Johannes, I was not around. Junior went out to the stream alone to trim out some trees. As he was working, he missed the branch he was trying to cut and sank the axe into his foot. He limped home bleeding and in extreme pain.

The closest doctor was the Johannes brother who had served as a medic in the Civil War. When he got the word, I was at the Johannes farm. We rushed to the Wagner farm. Junior was seriously hurt, bones were broken, but the foot could heal if there was no infection. Johannes washed his foot carefully, using the usual whiskey as an antiseptic. He carefully wrapped the foot in a tight bandage.

Three days later, it appeared that there was the beginning of an infection. Acting in frustration, Alfred called another doctor in the area. This doctor unwrapped the bandage, tried to set the injured bones and remove any infection. In the process, severe bleeding began. The doctor was unable to stop the bleeding.

I was not present and didn't want to be. I knew Junior would die, but not how. I was angry, not knowing if I could have saved him in any case. My biggest frustration was the modern medicine I knew about was not available that could have easily saved him.

The family was devastated. Christina had many losses in her life and would have many more. Junior's death would certainly contribute to Alfred's early demise a few years later.

Elsa, now in her thirties, seemed to age five years overnight. She always cared for the Wagner children as if they were her own.

Old obituaries often emphasized that people who died did not suffer long in part to make the survivors feel less miserable about their loss. It was also true that the dying generally did not suffer long because modern life-prolonging medicine and procedures were not available.

The scourges of the time found in Wisconsin for which there were no vaccines nor good treatments would have included small pox, typhoid, typhus, tuberculosis, diphtheria, scarlet fever, rheumatic fever, measles, mumps, chicken pox, gangrene, cholera, polio, syphilis, gonorrhea and various wound infections. Routine operations for appendicitis, gall bladder, joint surgeries, hernias and other repairable ailments were also not available.

I did my best to console the Wagners after the loss of Junior. For all the many positive things that people experienced at the time, frequent and sudden death was always a reality. I was happy to visit during the 1850s–1860s for my mission but would never have wanted to live my real life at that time given their lack of medical technology. Then again, I suppose the same could be said of every generation.

The loss of Junior was not just hard on the Wagners, but it made me even more frustrated about living in the past. Losing patience with the tragedies of the time, I felt that I was getting closer to the decision to return to my present life. Elsa and I were having unusual periods of silence when we were together. Both of us were sensing that changes were coming in our lives.

CHAPTER 47 – DISCUSSION

"How do you know if someone is right for you?" Elsa asked me one day. "Can a person ever find that perfect match?" Elsa appeared to be asking for my advice as if she were now looking elsewhere for a husband. She had every right to go down that road, but I was uncomfortable with the line of thought.

"You mean marriage?" I asked.

"Yes," she said. "What are the signs? Several marriages that I have seen are just not very good. Some of those people shouldn't be married. Divorce should be easier to get."

Elsa mentioned a man I didn't know who had committed suicide. "His wife had a sharp tongue," Elsa said. "He couldn't take it any longer. He should have walked out of the marriage."

"Look at the Zimmers," Elsa continued. "When the infant daughter died, the husband blamed the wife. Then she killed herself."

"That probably had more to do with not being able to deal with the tragedy," I replied. Men sometimes don't know how difficult it is for a woman to lose a little one."

"Some families seem to be cursed, plagued with bad luck!" I said hesitatingly without believing in curses or luck. "I can't explain it. But I agree with you. Some marriages should end. Life here is tough too. There is too much work and not enough fun as I see it."

"Do some people have demons?" Elsa asked.

"No, I don't believe in demons," I replied.

"But the Bible says there are demons," she continued.

"People in the Bible attributed demons to those who were mentally ill," I replied. "They had no other way to explain it. They didn't have the science and medicine we have now. Minds can be ill just like bodies."

"Do you believe in witches?" Elsa continued, venturing farther from the subject.

"No," I replied.

"What about magic?"

"These are things we don't understand, but science sooner or later usually has an explanation."

"Is there really such a thing as a one-and-only love?" Elsa continued, returning to her original query.

"It is hard to find a one-and-only," I replied. "It is a wonderful thought, but for most people, there may be no such person anywhere. Let's just look your chances for a perfect match in Centerville, for example," I ventured. "First, there is a relatively small number of potential partners to choose from in Centerville because it is a relatively small community to start with.

"Second, at your age, most of the eligible bachelors and the best choices are already married. You are left with the widowers or those who probably shouldn't be married.

"Third, you or your suitor can realistically only travel so far by horse to go dating, say ten or fifteen miles.

"Fourth, you have a significant number of close relatives in the community that you can't or shouldn't choose from.

"Fifth, cut whatever number you have in half because Catholics don't get to choose from Protestants and Protestants don't get to choose from Catholics.

"Sixth, cut that number in half again," I laughed. "Because of Lake Michigan, there is no east, so half of your prospective territory for finding a mate does not exist!

"You have to choose the best one available and then try to make it work," I concluded.

"Love is such an emotional thing when we are young," I continued. "Love becomes more practical and less romantic as we get older. One should never jump into a marriage too fast. The most solid relationships, one would think, would be between best friends, real soul mates.

"My measure of a good relationship," I asserted, "is whether what you do in life goes better when you are with that other person, or when you are alone. It's kind of like saying that in a good relationship, one plus one equals more than two.

"The problem I see is that there is too much family pressure on relationships and not enough experimentation available before marriage," I continued my lecture, not thinking again about the century I was in. "People should spend more time working together, studying together, enjoying music and sports, traveling together, even sharing secrets," I laughed.

"Are you suggesting sex before marriage?" Elsa asked. I was surprised that she mentioned this, given the taboos of the time.

"Risky," I replied. I considered mentioning birth control but couldn't since such things didn't realistically exist at the time. Elsa was ahead of her time, I realized, knowing that she was often on the fence trying to be both religious and liberated. She would probably like the future!

"So, do things go better with us when we are together?" Elsa demanded of me.

"Absolutely!" I had to answer.

"Do we share secrets?" Elsa smiled.

"We already have, right?" I replied.

"Are you my one-and-only?" she asked, looking me straight in the eye. Not answering, I hugged her again, as I often did, not wanting to let her go.

Chapter 48 – Future

Elsa challenged me. "Tell me, what is my future?" she demanded. "You are different, you know so much, you are not one of us, are you?"

I pondered that even if I knew the future, would it be fair to say anything? "Who really wants to know one's future?" I replied. "I can't help you because I just don't know," I lied. "I'm not a fortune-teller, seer or some type of wizard. I'm not God and won't try to play God!"

I became silent. Elsa, tough as she was, was crying. Now in her thirties, she was truly a spinster in most eyes. Elsa saw only loneliness ahead of her. She wanted a husband and children, a more normal existence.

However, after I would leave, I knew that she would hurry into an unhappy marriage and two years later, die in childbirth. I could not tell her that. There is no way I would want her to be hurt. As much as we decide much of our lives or think we do, can we escape our designated fate? Are we really in charge? Is there a plan somewhere? Does God exist or really care?

I grabbed Elsa and hugged her tightly. "I love you," I said. "I love you so much!"

"I love you too," she replied. "I just don't understand what is going on! I want to keep you."

"Can we get married?" she asked.

"I would marry you if I could," I replied.

"What's keeping you from marrying me?" Elsa demanded. "Is there something wrong with me? Am I not attractive? I beg you, I would do anything to keep you!"

It seemed that an hour of silence followed. I couldn't say anything. Elsa was so frustrated, I thought she was going to hit me.

I could read Elsa's thoughts. She continued to be concerned about what the public would think, that if she couldn't land me as a husband, as close as we were, she would never find anyone. It would confirm that there was really something wrong with her. She would be a failure, a loser. She would never be able to go back and face those local suitors again. I sometimes feared that Elsa would go crazy or attempt suicide like her brother.

Once again, I had to consider my decision. I could stay in the past and forfeit my future existence, something I wasn't even sure I would be allowed to do. Or I could bring Elsa to the future and deal with all of this then.

I had already decided. I was not going to stay in the past. I had seen what I needed to see. I needed to complete my future. My life story would not be finished in the past.

I finally had to tell Elsa what I could. "What I can promise is that I will see you again when this is all over," I stated firmly.

"Are we going to heaven?" she asked.

"Not exactly, something before heaven," I replied. "It is all that I can say. I have already said too much!"

Surprisingly Elsa, hugged me even harder and kissed me repeatedly.

"It's okay," she finally said. "I'll take what I can get. I'll do what you say. Apparently, I have no choice. In some ways, I really hate you!" she shouted.

"You must be an angel," she then said quietly. "I trust you! Please, please take me with you, if not now, then sometime soon!"

CHAPTER 49 – FAREWELL

I spent considerable time planning my departure. The year was 1870. I had spent a dozen years with my ancestors, longer than the few months I had planned, all because of Elsa. I had fulfilled my mission and a lot more. Elsa was going to alter my future.

Looking for a very good excuse to leave, I told the Wagners that I had decided to move back to Germany after all to work in the printing business with some people I had known in my village. I produced a fake letter to prove it. I quit my outside work to spend the final weeks with Elsa and the Wagners.

I played a lot with the kids, especially the two little girls, Tina, seven years old, and Melanie, five. Tina would become another victim of the times, dying after childbirth at 29. Her husband would marry again. Out of respect for Tina, her husband would decide to be buried next to both of his wives.

I would briefly remember Melanie who died when I was young. Like so many of the incredible things I experienced in my time travel, to meet someone as a child from the first Wagner generation born in

America and then to meet her again 90 years later was totally awesome!

I saw in Ludwig, my ancestor, a fierce determination to succeed. With his older brother now gone, he would be able to someday take the reins of the farm. It would come sooner than he hoped. Alfred would die when Ludwig was 16. Ludwig also had a bit of a temper.

"Why don't you take Elsa with you?" Alfred begged. "You two belong to each other."

Christina stated likewise that she wanted Elsa to be with me. Elsa, however, covering for me, stated quite firmly that she would not move back to Germany. "I am an American now. The Wagners are my family."

"I would find a way to visit you if I could," Alfred told me. "But my brother Herman has written to me several times that there is still a warrant for my arrest. I am always hoping that he may come to visit me in the not too distant future," Alfred pondered, looking off to the east.

I knew that Herman would never come.

"Please write to tell us how you are doing," Alfred continued.

Elsa cried in my embrace as we sat on the same stump we had used when I first met her. I did my best to console her. Elsa guessed by this time that I wasn't going to Germany.

"Why are you lying to us? Where are you really going? Is there something wrong with us?" she repeated.

All I could say was that I was going back to where I came from.

"You are not going to Germany!" she retorted. "Why, why, why are you doing this to me!"

"Elsa, you always knew I was different, that somehow, I didn't belong," I begged. "I am now proving it."

"Why did you come, then?"

"I came to see my ancestors and then God brought you to me!"

"You are an angel, I know it!" she shouted, not letting me respond. "Please act like one! Bring me some good news! Angels always bring good news!"

"Elsa, I am telling you again, we are not finished," I whispered in her ear. "We will meet again. I will eventually bring you to me. It is not Germany, it is not heaven. We can decide our future then. But for the moment, you must forgive me, you must forget me, you must move on. It is your destiny. It is my destiny. We are something very special. Never lose sight of that. Always remember that. What we have is just ours and nobody else's."

Elsa looked stunned, but relieved. "Can you really do it?" she asked.

"Yes!"

I gave Elsa a ring. "Never take this off!" I demanded.

"There is a dance tomorrow night," I reminded Elsa. "It is at the new dance hall in the village. I will leave after that. Please don't ask me any more questions now. I love you! I will always love you! Trust me!"

We did not interact with others at the dance and did not speak much to each other, just danced. People were eyeing us, realizing that something was very different.

"Maybe they are breaking up?" people seemed to think. Elsa would tell people later that I decided to move back to Germany. And that there was another man in her future.

On more than one occasion that last night, we embraced among the buggies outside. We hoped the night would never end. Back inside, they announced the Elsa Polka.

"They are playing our music," I said. "Let's go back in!"

PART TWO

Chapter 50 – Reunion

I picked Elsa up at the airport. We were somewhat older now. We were surprised to see that we had aged but got over it in a moment. "I guess we couldn't expect to be young after what we have been through," she smiled, speaking in English.

"It's good to see you in the flesh," I replied, as I held Elsa tightly. Not completely trusting in the science of retrieving someone from the past, I was delighted that she was not a hologram or other humanoid pretension. She was the real Elsa as far as I could tell. We kissed and hugged for several minutes.

"I love you so much!" we both said simultaneously.

"Welcome to the present! Welcome to the future! We are together again!" I almost shouted.

"So, you were finally able to bring me here!" Elsa stated gleefully, constantly looking around. "What year is it?"

"It's the year 2000."

It's been that long?" Elsa looked shocked. "So, you came to see me from this time?" It's more than a hundred years!"

"I really came to see you several years ago. Sorry for the wait, but I didn't know until recently when or how you were coming back," I replied. We each had a mission and fortunately a lot of help from advanced science. "I can't explain it, honest," I said. "Someone must have decided that this was the time, perhaps because I am now retired, perhaps because I now have the financial resources to help you, perhaps because my research into the Wagner past has reached a critical point."

Elsa sat quiet for a few moments, trying to take it all in, rubbing the ring on her finger that I gave her in 1870. "I can't believe this," she gasped.

"It seems like a dream, doesn't it? Maybe this is a dream!" Elsa said.

"You still have the ring I gave you," I said happily. "It connects you to me from there to here. This is not a dream!" I grabbed Elsa's hand and touched the ring.

"But God certainly had a hand in it?" Elsa continued, maintaining her core beliefs.

"No contact with God that I am aware of," I said. "But when you time-travel or bring people from the dead, you almost need to believe in divine intervention. We still needed to live out our lives."

"But am I not on my second life?" Elsa shouted. "You could have at least brought me back before I died! Dying is no fun, you know!"

People at the airport who were initially happy to glimpse our wonderful reunion were now eyeing us suspiciously.

"Elsa, you need to speak more quietly," I whispered. "When I was with you, I couldn't bring you with me to the future. I could have stayed, but then we wouldn't be here today. We would both be dead. It's complicated."

"Elsa, I have something important I need to tell you right now. My name is not Otto Hamann. It is Otto Wagner. I am actually the great-great grandson of Alfred and Christina. I used the name Hamann when I came to see the Wagners to hide my real identity."

Elsa at first looked surprised, but then smiled. "I never believed half of what you told me anyway! You were an angel then and I hope that you still are!"

"Thank you!" I replied. "There is much to explain that you will soon understand."

Anticipating Elsa's old wardrobe, I brought some modern clothes for her. I smiled at Elsa's old clothes. "You look like you did in the 1860s."

People were staring at her as if she were an old-order Mennonite. Elsa saw women wearing pants. Others wearing short skirts.

"No way!" she exclaimed. "No pants. Long dress, please! How can women dress like that?"

"Don't worry, I said. "I got something appropriate for you."

Elsa changed in the ladies' restroom. It took her a while to emerge.

"What were you doing in there?" I asked. "The clothes didn't fit?"

Elsa admitted to flushing a toilet about ten times, playing with the automatic water faucets and waving out the paper towels.

"Those things are wonderful! Where does the dirty water go?" she demanded.

"It goes through a pipe to a sewage treatment plant where it is cleaned and returned to nature," I said.

Elsa saw a television monitor in the airport. She stood fascinated. "Is this thing truly alive?" she asked. "Are those people in this building?"

"No, those people are talking right now from many parts of the world," I replied. "Plus, some of what you see has been recorded earlier."

"Recorded?"

"I'll explain later."

Chapter 51 – Renewal

"I hope you have had a good life," Elsa said, relaxing a bit.

"Well, I am divorced," I replied. "But otherwise life has been generally good."

"Was your wife anything like me?" Elsa asked with a smile. "Of course, she was like me," Elsa continued. "She was too much for you!"

"No, there is no one like you!" I blurted. "It would have been unfair to expect her to be anyone other than who she was."

"But it didn't work out?" Elsa asked.

"No. In my mind, knowing that you were returning to see me did cast a shadow over my marriage."

"I'm sorry about that," Elsa moaned. "Should I go back?"

"Never!"

"Will I get to meet her?" Elsa continued.

"If you wish," I replied. "However, it might be more than a little uncomfortable!"

"Any children?"

"Yes, two daughters, Sarah and Jennifer. Sarah is married."

"Will I meet them?"

"Of course!"

"Any grandchildren?"

"Two, another on the way."

"Will you tell Sarah and Jennifer about me?"

"Not initially," I concluded. "But I think they should know the truth someday. For the moment, what we have accomplished would cause too much trouble for us if others knew."

"Our time-travel secret will eventually be known by others," I continued. "In fact, I'm sure that others are already doing it. Perhaps my daughters or grandchildren will also want to time-travel. We will all eventually want to move back and forth between the past and the present. It would be nice to avoid death altogether. Science is working on this. But then the world would quickly fill up."

"There are so many people?" Elsa wondered.

"Almost seven billion," I said. "Not millions, but billions!"

"I don't understand that number!" Elsa replied.

"Your work?" Elsa went back to asking about me.

"I recently retired from my work as a university professor," I replied. "Remember when you met me in the garden and wished that I were a nobleman or a professor? Well, I couldn't tell you at the time that I was indeed a professor from the future. Sorry, I'm not a 'blueblood' though, not of royal descent. I don't have a fancy title, nor do I own a castle!"

"But you have a doctorate degree?" Elsa stated.

"Yes."

"So, you do have a title, Doctor Otto!"

I recalled our first meeting. "It was in a garden where I was tempted by the maid!" I laughed. "How Biblical! You didn't bring me crashing down into a state of original sin, but you sure complicated my mission! And how lucky I was that you did!"

"Let's talk about you," I said.

"I didn't have much of a life after you left as I'm sure you already know," Elsa said. "My husband Karl was a nice man. But he couldn't understand me and my relationship to you. And I couldn't explain it either, of course."

"I'm sorry about that," I apologized. "I only met Karl once when we worked on the Census. I did not know that you would marry him."

"I will tell you everything about him later," Elsa continued. "I have so many questions. But I too am so happy to have this second chance! I still can't believe that this is really happening!"

"What happened to my daughter Anita?" Elsa said suddenly. Elsa had survived only a week after Anita's birth.

"Anita was brought up by your husband and his sister," I replied. "After a slow start without you, Anita turned out to be strong and healthy and lived a long life. She married a man named Lawrence Schneider from Manitowoc. They had a daughter Edna and a son Oscar. Then they moved to Milwaukee. I don't know where Anita and her husband are buried. I was going to do more of the research before you came but didn't get to it. We can find out."

"I know that Oscar moved to California to work," I continued. "He never married and has died. However, Edna still lives in Milwaukee. She is very old. She is your granddaughter."

"Can we see her today?"

"Not today, she is two hours away," I replied. "Be patient, it will be soon. We need to think more about meeting her."

"How did the Wagners accept my departure in 1870?" I asked, changing the subject.

"They were very sad, but like me, they seemed to think you were an angel. They didn't talk much about you after you left. Nobody else talked about you either. It was as if you were intended to leave without a trace."

"Was I an angel or a ghost?" I laughed.

"Both!"

We sat silently for a while looking out of the window at the airplanes.

"This is now your mission," I told Elsa.

She then told me that she thought she was mentally prepared to see the modern world but was nonetheless totally overwhelmed.

"No one can be prepared for all the changes that would have occurred in a century and a half," I assured her.

When Elsa died, there was no automobile, telephone, electric power, airplane, radio, television, video, computer, internet, antibiotic, plastic, nor atomic bomb. Neither was there any income tax, social security, health insurance, life insurance, crop insurance, nor a woman's right to vote.

"Just be patient," I told her. "Don't try to absorb everything at once."

"But, isn't this really heaven?" Elsa had to ask again.

"No, the world is just more advanced in many ways than it was before," I replied. "Every day something new is discovered or invented."

"But God must have made these things!" she said. "People could not do it!'

"But they did," I stated. "We have much more science and knowledge than you did in your time."

"And you didn't tell me about all of these things when you came?" Elsa laughed.

"How could I?" I replied. "No one would have believed me. People need time to adjust to change. Some never do. That's why we need new generations."

"Do people leave the earth?" Elsa then asked. "Do these airplanes leave?"

"No, but things called rockets do. A few people have landed on the moon."

"You must be kidding!"

"Some rockets have landed on other planets."

"With people?"

"Not yet."

"Can we go to the moon?"

"Realistically, no. Such travel takes special training. It would be very expensive."

"What about doctors, medicine? Would I have been saved when I had my baby?" Elsa wondered.

"I don't know all the details about your giving birth," I replied. "But I would say it's very likely that you would have survived. Medicine now can save many people from illness and injury that would not have been cured back then. Friedrich, baby Hans, baby Emily, Emma, Junior, Tina, you, and even Alfred himself would very likely have lived longer today."

"Emma and Tina did not live long?"

"No," I replied. "Both died in childbirth like you did."

"Do people now live to be one-hundred?" Elsa continued.

"Some I replied, but the average life expectancy is now in the seventies or eighties as compared to the fifties in your time."

"You have all these wonderful machines and medicines," Elsa asked. "So why can't people live to be a thousand years old?"

"We are far from that. Biology is more complicated than mechanical technology."

"But didn't Jesus come back?" Elsa blurted, changing the subject back to religion. "The ministers all said that Jesus was coming soon, that the world was so full of sin, that we were living in the end of times!"

"Theologians say that all the time, what the end is near," I replied. "No Jesus yet. Sorry, but we have not seen Him."

"But are there still Christians?" Elsa asked.

"Yes, there are millions of them."

"Does God talk to them?"

"I haven't heard of it," I said.

"Has God forgotten us?"

"We need to give Him more time," I said, not wanting to say that I doubted many of the promises of religion.

Regarding a world full of sin, Elsa had seen nothing yet, I considered. She could not have imagined in her time, that apart from the horrors of the Civil War, the brutal subjection and genocide of the Native Americans, the conquest of Africa and other bad things, these were somehow small in sheer numbers in comparison to the sins of the 20th century ahead of her. Between the surrender of Napoleon in 1815 and the outbreak of the first world war, the Europe that Elsa left enjoyed a near century of relative peace. There were numerous treaties, fledgling democracies, the formal abolition of slavery, incredible advances in science, literature, music and philosophy, and so forth. Then all hell broke loose in 1914. I would explain the 20th century to Elsa later.

CHAPTER 52 – TRAVEL

"I'm ready to leave. How do we move from here?" Elsa asked.

"I have a car, an automobile," I replied.

Elsa saw people driving them up to the doorways. "I want to see one."

"You will ride in one!" I laughed.

"How far are we from Centerville?"

"About one hour."

"How many miles?"

"About sixty miles."

"Sixty miles in one hour?"

"Yes."

"Are there any horses and buggies left?"

"Very few, not on the roads we will be on."

We walked toward the parking lot. I had to watch that Elsa didn't step into the path of a car. Then suddenly she was afraid to cross the street even if a car was far away or pedestrians had the right-of-way.

"Right-of-way?" Elsa asked. "There are lights telling us when to walk? Lights telling cars when to stop? Incredible!"

"You still need to be careful," I insisted.

I got Elsa into the passenger seat. "Fasten your seat belt," I ordered.

"What is that?"

I had to help her with the seatbelt.

"Are we going to crash?"

"No."

"Maybe I should sit in the back and not look."

"No, you will be just fine sitting up front."

"Please don't go too fast!" Elsa pleaded. "Can I jump out if I am afraid?"

"No way, you will be seriously injured or die if you do! I will lock the doors."

"Oh, I am afraid already!"

"I need to call someone," I said suddenly, reaching for my phone. Elsa stared at me and the phone.

"You're kidding!" she said. "I heard rumors of this invention, but never saw it, she continued."

I had to call my daughter Jennifer in Madison to tell her to feed my house cat for a few extra days. I then gave the phone to Elsa. She briefly spoke to Jennifer. After she finished, she looked at all the buttons on the phone.

"I will explain those tomorrow," I said.

"Does the voice travel through the air?"

"Yes."

Elsa liked the ride. I tried to explain all the gadgets in the car. Elsa was, of course, very curious about everything she was seeing.

After some time, she said, "Can we go faster?"

"No, there is a speed limit. I will point out those signs along the road. It is not safe to drive too fast. And the police may stop me and give me a fine."

"I don't see any police."

"They hide in cars. They have machines that can tell how fast I am going."

"Can this machine fly?"

"No."

Elsa was amazed by the size of the highways, by the idea that cars could be traveling peacefully on overpasses over other cars. "There are so many cars! What are those big cars?"

"Those are trucks."

"Do they carry many people?"

"No, they carry cargo, just things, not people. Did you see the bus at the airport?" I asked. "Those buses are big cars that carry people. You can tell buses are for people because they have many windows for people to look out."

"What are all those big signs for?" Elsa asked.

"Those are called billboards," I replied. "They are used by businesses to advertise their products and services."

"But there are so many!" Elsa said. "They confuse me. I don't understand their language. And I think they make the countryside look ugly."

"I'm sorry," she continued. "They are colorful, but truly ugly. Many people would agree with you," I replied. "Billboards are part of the price we pay for our capitalism."

"Capitalism? You mean the system that Marx hated?"

"You are definitely up on your reading," I laughed at Elsa.

"What are all those wires for?" Elsa asked, looking overhead.

"Mostly for carrying electricity."

"What does electricity do?"

"Electricity powers many of the machines you see."

"But there are no wires attached to the cars? How does electricity move in a wire anyway?"

Elsa was asking too many questions for me to keep up.

"Cars run on gasoline but do have electrical systems in them," I continued. "Cars can also store electricity in a battery. Some newer cars run entirely on electricity stored in batteries. I will show you the engine and other parts of this car later."

"So many things to explain!" I muttered to myself.

"But aren't those wires also ugly?" Elsa said.

"Yes, they are," I replied. "We are putting some of them underground. But I look forward to the day when we don't need wires. I take a lot of photographs and don't like wires in my photos. Nor billboards!"

I turned on the car radio. Elsa was delighted.

"Before I died, there were people who imagined such a device," she said. "Can we find polka music?"

"Probably not on the radio," I replied. "But I have something called a CD, an abbreviation for a compact disc," I explained.

I allowed Elsa to hold the CD and had her put it in the slot. "Let me find our song," I said, as I pushed the button to the Elsa Polka, recorded by the grandson of the orchestra leader she knew. Elsa started to cry and then hugged me tightly.

"Don't distract my driving," I laughed. "We can hug later."

"Please, now!" she shouted.

"Let me get off the road first." I pulled over and we hugged, both in tears, for about ten minutes as we listened to our song several times. "This is truly amazing," Elsa said.

"Let's listen to some other music," I said. I happened to have Johann Strauss, John Phillip Souza, Moody Blues, and Willie Nelson on board. I picked out a CD by 10,000 Maniacs, an all-female group, something I knew Elsa would like to hear about. I had to explain why musical groups used such strange names.

"We'll try Led Zeppelin later," I laughed to myself.

Elsa was almost raptured by the Strauss waltzes. "I knew this music before I died!" she cried. "The polka band first played it. Then the minister played it on his violin in church. Karl and I attended a concert in Manitowoc that featured Strauss music. This is the most beautiful music in the world!"

"I agree," I replied. "We are both Germans, so this type of music runs in our blood. Strauss was an Austrian," I added. "But close enough to us."

There was always an attraction for me to the rhythm of waltzes, I realized. Perhaps it was because I was exposed to waltzes played by polka bands at a young age. Although I love many types of music, waltzes by Johann Strauss reach my German soul like none other.

I told Elsa that I would expose her to many types of music. Then at some point I would ask her opinion about her favorites. It would not take her long to like the Moody Blues.

Chapter 53 – Cleveland

We arrived in Cleveland, the village that had incorporated Hika and that Elsa knew briefly before she died. Elsa was intently staring in every direction, at every landmark. She didn't hear me ask her about lunch.

"Are you hungry?" I asked again.

"Can we go to the Wagner farm to eat?" she eventually asked. "Are they waiting for me? Do the Wagners still own the farm?" Elsa suddenly fretted.

"Yes, my nephew owns it."

"We will eat at a restaurant," I insisted. I had only briefly explained Elsa's visit to my nephew at the Wagner farm and had made no firm arrangements yet. We first had to be careful how to introduce her so as not to cause a problem. "We will stay at a motel, a type of inn, tonight," I said. "We will visit the Wagner farm tomorrow or the next day."

We both ordered a hamburger. Although Elsa had seen a meat grinder and had tasted ground meat, she had never seen or tasted anything like the modern version of a hamburger. She really liked it. Elsa liked the ketchup and the fries too. I told her to regard a hamburger as a treat rather than a basic meal.

"Why?" she asked.

"Hamburgers and fries are not a balanced diet. People need more vegetables and fruits in their diets."

"Are hamburgers and fries the reason why so many people are fat?" she asked, having already commented on the many obese people she was seeing.

"There are many reasons for obesity," I replied.

Elsa was shocked by the bill. "You shouldn't pay this. These people are crooks to charge so much!"

"It isn't much," I tried to explain. "Prices go up over time. Ten dollars would have bought you five acres in your time, but now it buys two hamburgers. It's called inflation. We also earn more money now."

"How much?" Elsa asked.

"When I was working, I earned over $50,000 a year."

"You are joking! You must be a millionaire!"

"I never got that far," I laughed. "I spent most of it. Not on hamburgers either! My car cost me $5,000 and it was old when I bought it."

We first drove through the Village of Cleveland to Hika on the lakeshore. Elsa recognized the New Settlement Tavern and the former inn, now a residence. There were a few houses around the village that she knew. Elsa pointed out the locations of businesses in Hika no longer in existence. "The brewery was there, the sawmill there, the general store there," she said.

"There was a beer cave next to the brewery," Elsa said pointing, somewhere over there." Where she pointed was now under a street intersection. It confirmed what I had heard about its location, but no one was about to dig up an intersection just to find an old beer cave.

"Lake Michigan is definitely higher," Elsa added. I pointed out a few of the posts remaining from one of the old piers.

"We used to walk to a place out there just to get our feet wet," she pointed. It was now too deep to walk in.

We went into the New Settlement Tavern. I cautioned Elsa not to reveal anything about her past. "It is different inside," Elsa said quietly. "But, certainly the same building. I'm happy that some things from my past are still here."

"You will probably not see much," I interjected. "Don't be shocked! You can't imagine how much has disappeared just in my lifetime."

We spent some time looking at the old photos of the village on the walls, taken after her time, but showing scenes, buildings and even people that she knew. Deflecting any potential questions about Elsa's comments, I told the curious patrons that we were thinking about doing an updated history of the village.

We walked around the former sites of the two churches in Hika. Only the Catholic church parsonage was still there, now a private home. We talked to the owner. I introduced Elsa as a long-lost cousin.

We entered the Hika Cemetery, now a single unit with the Lutheran and Catholic sections combined. "Gennie was buried over there," Elsa said, pointing to the corner.

We walked to the grave. The stone was still legible. Elsa also pointed to the gravestones of Lutheran-Catholic couple once separated by a fence. "I'm glad the fence is gone," she said.

We looked at several stones of people she knew in her lifetime. "I knew he wouldn't live very long," she said, looking at one stone. "He spent more time in the tavern than at home!" "I heard that the father of that man cut him out of his will, leaving his inheritance to his grandchildren." I said.

Between the two of us we were able to reconstruct the stories of several of the people buried there.

"Can we bring these people to the present?" Elsa wondered. "I need to talk to them."

"It is not our mission," I replied. "Someday we will be able to do it," I assured her.

We then drove to the dance hall where we danced our last dance in 1870. The building was much the same. We got permission from the owner to walk around inside.

Suddenly we both had visions of ghosts from the past, that the hall was full of happy people dancing and drinking. We could hear them talking and laughing. We could almost touch them. The music was very loud. The floor shook beneath us with the impact of the dancing. It was a very strange and wonderful experience! It was like a dream come alive. And then the place went quiet again. We looked at each other for a moment and then laughed.

CHAPTER 54 – GRAVE

We then visited the cemetery where Elsa was buried north of Cleveland on the border between the Centerville and Newton townships. It was her husband's home church cemetery. The church was no longer there. Elsa pointed out its former location. "We attended that church before we married and I moved to Manitowoc," she said. "We were married in it." Elsa paused for a few minutes to reflect on her memories.

"Why do they tear down churches?" Elsa wondered aloud.

"They get old, too small, too expensive to maintain, or too expensive to repair," I replied. "Maybe the congregation dies out. Sometimes smaller churches combine to form a larger one. Sometimes there is a shortage of ministers in my bellysters."

"But the churches I knew were beautiful, very precious!" Elsa said.

I had to tell Elsa that her gravestone was in the old cemetery across the road. She was taken aback. I figured that she may or may not have known where she was buried.

"I did not make any arrangements because I was not planning to die," Elsa moaned. "Toward the end, I remember feeding little Anita. I had a fever, an infection in my belly. I was very weak. The last thing I remember was thinking that I was just going to sleep for a while. I told Karl to wake me in an hour. I squeezed his hand. I never woke up. There was a feeling of immense peace. I remember seeing a bright light!

It was astounding to listen to Elsa recounting the story of her death. Other than near-death experiences, no one can tell us what the last part of dying was really like.

I knew that Elsa would not be happy with what she saw at the cemetery. She did not know where her stone was. At the time of her untimely death, no spot would have yet been chosen.

I located the stone for her. It was not the original. Apparently, the original stone, made of limestone, not marble or granite, had weathered to the point of not being legible. A relative replaced it, misspelled the last name, and got the death year wrong. I thought about replacing it myself but wanted Elsa to see it.

Elsa cried. "Is this all that is left of my memory? They can't even get the information on the stone right! It's such a small stone too. It is even sinking into the ground. No flowers. No one remembers me!"

"It is the fate of most of us," I replied regretfully.

Elsa hugged her gravestone for several minutes, sobbing. You can't imagine what it was like to see a woman crying on her own grave!

"Can we come back later?" she asked as she recovered. "I need to think about fixing this."

"I will help you do it," I assured her. "You will get a new stone."

"Where is Karl buried?"

"He is buried with his first wife in Manitowoc in the large cemetery on the south side of the city," I replied. "I have not seen the stone. It may be hard to locate in such a large cemetery. We will check with the cemetery record office first."

"I know you will ask why Karl was not buried with you," I continued. "I'm not sure, but I think he wanted you to be closer to the Wagner farm. His children from his first marriage would have had a decision in that too."

Elsa admitted that she was not as close to his children as she might have wanted to be. "The children were married and moved away when I came along. But why didn't he bury me with the Wagners on the Saxon Cemetery?"

Chapter 55 – Motel

Suddenly, Elsa said that she was very exhausted. No surprise, I thought, with what she has been going through.

"Where are we staying?" Elsa asked.

"Let's stay at a motel near Manitowoc," I suggested. "I know a good place. We can have some privacy there."

"Can you find my house in Manitowoc?" she asked.

"I don't know the house, or even if it is still there," I replied.

"Do you know the address?"

"No, but you would know the street. We can go there tomorrow before we go to the Wagner farm."

At the motel, I asked for separate rooms. Elsa smiled at me and politely complained about the bill, cheap by my standards, still shocking to her. "Separate rooms," I insisted to the manager.

We went to a sports bar to eat. She asked for another hamburger. I insisted that she have a small salad with it. She also tried a beer. We talked about plans for tomorrow.

Elsa was quickly getting used to some of things she was seeing.

She couldn't keep her eyes off the television.

"What game is that?"

"Football," I replied.

"Are they supposed to fight with each other?"

"No, that is called tackling."

"But it's so rough, don't some of them die?"

"No, but they do often get hurt. Some of them suffer later from head injuries."

"Do they still play stick ball?" Elsa asked.

"Well, it's called baseball now."

"I wanted to play that game, but the men wouldn't let me," Elsa said. "I used to hit stones with a stick when the Wagners weren't home. One day I left my seat at a game in Hika, walked onto the field, grabbed a bat and stood in the box. The men laughed at me. One of them shouted to give me an easy pitch. I hit the ball over everyone's head and went back to my seat."

"Should I have been born a boy?" Elsa wondered.

"You were a modern woman," I laughed. "Millions of men today would like you to be just the type of woman you are."

"Are you one of them?" Elsa stared lovingly at me.

"The one first in line!" I smiled, and then kissed her across the table.

Elsa seemed to be overly impressed by the television commercials. "That sounds like a good idea," she would say. "Why don't you buy it?"

"It's just advertising," I replied. "You can't believe half of what they say. You are just vulnerable because you haven't seen television advertising before. Remember the snake oil salesmen of your day? It's the same thing."

We went back to the motel. I slowly kissed Elsa goodnight in the hallway, helped her turn on her television, and turned in. I couldn't sleep, thinking about Elsa, our first day, and what would happen tomorrow.

I thought about our new reality. Like Elsa, I couldn't believe what was happening.

I turned on my television, hoping to distract myself. Then there was a knock on the door. It was Elsa.

CHAPTER 56 – MANITOWOC

It was hard to get started in the morning after our night together. We stayed in until almost noon, reserved a single room for the following night, and had a late breakfast. Elsa needed some time to process what she was seeing.

In the afternoon, we hunted for Elsa's old house in Manitowoc and that of her best friend Nanette. Elsa's house was gone, replaced by a shop. Even the neighbor's houses had given way to businesses or parking lots.

Nanette's house was still there but had been remodeled to a large extent. The owners, a young couple, happened to be at home. They had no clue as to the history of the house but were welcoming. Elsa recognized their last name as a Manitowoc family of the past. "Our families have always lived here," was their response.

Elsa asked for a tour of the house, lying that a friend's grandmother had once lived there. She suddenly paused at the door of one of the rooms. It was the room where Elsa sat holding Nanette's hand when she died. Elsa excused herself, asked to use the bathroom, cried for a moment, composed herself and came back.

Elsa said quietly to me, "We should leave. I'm having a hard time with this."

We visited Nanette's grave in Manitowoc. Again, it was very difficult for Elsa. "Can we bring her to the future?" she asked. "Nanette really deserved a better life."

"It is not part of the mission," I replied. "Perhaps in the future. Most people would want and deserve another better life," I continued.

I considered a friend's quote about how many of us spend our time on this earth. "Too many people live out their lives in quiet desperation," he once said.

We drove to see the gravestone of Romy Gosz, the famous polka band leader buried in a Francis Creek cemetery. The stone listed Romy as "Roman L. Gosz" and had a trumpet engraved on it. We reminisced about the history of Bohemian music in Centerville. Our car parked in front of his grave, I put in the CD of Romy's music, including the Elsa polka.

I delayed the visit to the Wagner farm until the next morning. We spent a casual rest of the day walking along the lakeshore in Two Rivers reminiscing, laughing, hugging, kissing. I spent considerable time getting Elsa caught up on history, not only of the family, but also of the world.

Elsa was surprised, if not shocked, by much of what she learned about the world. "It seems like we keep repeating the same stupid things," Elsa continued. "Don't people ever learn anything from the past?"

I showed Elsa a world map that I always carried in my car. "Having a world map in your car says something about you!" she smiled.

"I drive locally but plan globally," I laughed.

"What has all happened?" she shouted, looking at the map. "Look at America! All the territories are now states. She counted them. There are 48!"

"You missed Alaska and Hawaii," I told her. "There are also some territories in the oceans."

Elsa then looked at Europe. "Poor Germany!" she said. "They lost a lot of territory. What happened? I really feel bad about Germany," she continued. "Germans are not bad people."

"Well, the Germans caused plenty of deaths and destruction," I countered. I quickly explained the World Wars and my visits to Auschwitz and Dachau. Elsa was shocked. I realized that it would take a long time before she could fully comprehend the history that had transpired after she died.

"But Germany is once again powerful, both economically and politically, just not militarily," I said.

"Look at Africa!" Elsa continued. Are all those real countries?"

"Yes, they are."

"Do they have buildings and cars and telephones?"

"Yes, you would be surprised at how far Africa has come since the 1870s."

"What languages do they speak?" she asked.

"They typically speak a national language depending on the largest tribe or ethnic group, and on the colonial power that conquered them, like English, French, Arabic or Portuguese. However, there are thousands of tribes that speak thousands of languages. Some of those are also national languages."

"What if I want to stay here with you?" Elsa asked suddenly.

"I thought that you might not like this modern life and all the things that have been forgotten from your time," I replied. "I was afraid that you would want to hurry back to your old path to immortality. You will have to leave unless you declare to stay. If you stay, you will die again. You will have to take another identity, establish another path."

"I'm beginning to think that I really want to stay," Elsa said. "This is my second chance to be with you, and I don't want to lose you again, even if we are older."

"We'll give it more time," I replied, realizing more and more that we could not leave each other again. "Let's go to a movie tonight."

Chapter 57 – Return

The next morning, we finally drove to the Wagner Farm. Elsa, like me in 1858, needed a few days to get up the courage to see the farm. I told her that I had called the owner, my nephew David Schneider.

We stopped on the road near the farm and got out of the car to give Elsa time to take in what she saw. It was the very same spot where I stood in 1858 when I first saw the Wagner farm. Elsa was silent but shaking with anticipation. So many memories were going through her head. I held her and told her about my thoughts when I first gazed at the farm in 1858. After about five minutes, Elsa indicated that she was ready.

David stayed home from work to meet us. He was working on a project in the shed. Being careful not to give away Elsa's real identity, I introduced her as a distant cousin from another state. I told David that Elsa's knowledge of the farm came mostly from me and one of her ancestors who had visited the farm in the late 1800s.

The farm land was now rented out to neighbors. A ranch house built in the early 1970s had replaced the 1871 frame house built by Alfred Wagner. The barn, granary, milk house, pig barn, smokehouse, garage and silos, were all structures that came after Elsa had died. No building survived from the 1870s. The orchards were also gone.

I asked David if Elsa and I could walk around the farm by ourselves. "Of course! he said, "Be my guest. You were born here after all," he said. "You know a lot more about this place than I do."

I wanted Elsa to be free to give me her honest tour out of earshot of David, filling me in on things that I may not have seen during my mission in the mid-1800s.

David was in his mid-thirties. Like most people his age, he was too busy with a job and family to be caught up on his local history. David seemed only mildly interested in the history of the farm. Understanding this, I took it upon myself over time to write down as much as I could about the farm and community. Elsa applauded my efforts. She would help me, she said.

Elsa was disappointed that the Meyer graves were no longer marked. We stood for a moment on the spot.

"I have given thought to moving the remains to the Saxon Cemetery," I replied. "I bought an extra plot just in case. I guessed that the softer bones of the infant Hans probably no longer existed. However, so long as the family owns the farm, I think the remains are safe where they are."

Elsa asked me if I had thought about an extra plot next to me for her. "It is a bit early to think about that!" I laughed. "But I do have an extra plot. My ex-wife would not want to be buried next to me!" I pondered the strange possibility of Elsa being buried in two places.

"But if the Wagner farm gets developed, some construction project may cover up or even dig up the Meyer graves," I said.

"Don't they respect burial sites?" Elsa asked.

"Not if they don't know they are there," I replied. The Meyer graves were not registered with the historical society. I tried to do that at one point, but they didn't seem to know how to do it. "I have some questions with the historical society, the Meyer graves being one of them," I complained.

We examined the cobblestones in the cow yard where the housebarn had once stood. The Wagners moved into the frame house that was started in 1871 when Elsa still lived with them. We shared our memories of that frame house in which I also grew up. The room Elsa once slept in was the same one that my brother and I slept in. "Elsa and I have too many ironic and spiritual connections for all of this to just be coincidental," I thought. "God continues to play with us!"

The housebarn was removed later when the large barn was built. Inside the large barn we could find several recycled beams. Only those beams, the cobblestones, the unmarked graves, and the well under the milk house remained as evidence of the original Wagner farm.

Elsa was amazed by the two old stone and brick silos, built in 1900 and 1910. I published a monograph on old county silos for the historical society. The Wagner stone silo built in 1900 was the oldest one that I could get a date for, although I figured a few older ones may have once existed in the county. Upright silos were introduced in Wisconsin in the 1880s.

Elsa pointed to a spot in the middle of the farm yard where the first milk house had once stood. In my time, we knew nothing of the building until we dug a trench for a water pipe and hit a buried concrete base.

We walked out to the woods. There was a pond now near where Junior's accident occurred. The boundary of the woods, now 16 acres in size, was farther west than Elsa had known. I explained that about 12 acres of the woods going west from the pond to the present boundary were removed in the 1880s to build the large barn and other structures.

Elsa asked to walk back to the homestead along the perimeter fence on the north side of the farm. The original farm had been 80 acres. An additional 40 acres on the north side was purchased by Christina in the 1870s after Alfred died.

Elsa commented on the barbed wire fence, something she had never seen. I commented that barbed wire was invented to contain cattle and other livestock but was probably more often used to contain humans. I referred to prisons, concentration camps, border divisions and other uses.

When we got to the midpoint of the fence from west to east, there were two posts together and the wires suddenly were fastened on the neighbor's side of the fence.

"Why are the wires on one side and then the other?" Elsa asked.

"It's the fencing law," I replied. "Each neighbor is responsible for half of the fence. So, we attach the wires on our side of the fence for our half and the neighbor does the same for his side. It is much easier to maintain your part of the fence with the wires and staples on your side. Cattle are less likely to push and damage the fence if the wires are nailed on their side. Cattle pushing on backside of the wires can eventually push staples out.

"But the wires are falling down here," Elsa said. "And there is no fence on the south side of the property. Neither is there any fencing for fields."

"The Wagners and the neighbors haven't kept cattle on the land in recent years, so the fences have fallen into disrepair," I replied. "Other than a few posts to mark the boundary, we don't need fences."

"So where do farmers keep the cattle?" she continued. I explained that many dairy cattle were now kept in confinement on fewer larger farms.

"There are some graziers around who still put their cattle on grass, like the Kaisers," I said.

"We need to visit the Kaisers," Elsa said. "I am happy they are still farming. They were good neighbors. We worked together with them often."

"We will certainly visit them," I assured Elsa. "We will visit both grazing and confinement farms."

"Which system do you like better, the grazing farms or the confinement farms?" Elsa asked.

"I definitely prefer the grazing farms," I replied.

Elsa asked what photos I had of the family and the farm.

"I have some at my house in Madison," I replied. "However, I donated most of my photo albums to the new Centreville Settlement Library."

"Where is it?" she asked.

"Just north of the Leitner housebarn," I replied. "We will go there tomorrow."

"How is the housebarn?" Elsa asked.

"It was restored and is now a museum. We will tour it too. I am a founder and lifetime member of the organization that restored it. I even have my own key to get in."

"Why was the Leitner housebarn not torn down?" Elsa asked.

"The housebarn never got in the way of other building projects," I said. "Plus, it is so large and sturdy that it would take some effort and cost to remove it. In later years, the Leitners opted to work in a factory instead of expanding the dairy herd like most other farmers in the neighborhood. Their dairy herd was maintained with the help of a hired man.

"I'm know the Leitners appreciated the historical value of housebarn," I replied. "The Kaisers and others emphasized to the Leitners at one point just how precious the building was. I've seen too many historical buildings pushed aside by development. Thankfully, the housebarn survived."

Chapter 58 – Restoration

In the afternoon we visited the Leitner housebarn and the library. Elsa spent considerable time in each room of the housebarn, recalling parties, conversations and other events. "Amanda and several other Leitner children were born in this room," she said as we toured the building.

At one point, Elsa was again showing some tears. "This is the room where I played with the children when the men built the barn. We had so much fun in here!"

"The housebarn is now on the National Register of Historical Places," I told Elsa.

"What does that mean?" she asked.

"It means that it is recognized by the National Park Service of the US Government as historically important."

"So that people won't destroy it?"

"The designation will not guarantee its survival but will certainly give ample reason to preserve it," I replied.

We looked at the panoramic, black and white photo of the Leitner descendants on one of the housebarn walls that was taken in 1924. The photo commemorated the 75th anniversary year of the arrival of the Leitner ancestors from Germany. Although the original couple had died long before as well as a dozen or so descendants, all the over 200 remaining descendants still lived in the area. There were 196 people in the photo, including several Wagners.

"My father was there, aged three." I pointed him out. The photo was, in my estimation, the most famous one ever taken in Town Centerville. Even when I was growing up, there were still 100 members of the Lutheran church in Cleveland who were Leitner descendants.

CHAPTER 59 – LIBRARY

We spent two hours in the library. There was an entire room dedicated to my collection of photo albums. "I am very proud of that," I mentioned.

"You did a mountain of work," Elsa said.

Elsa was thrilled about the idea of the library. However, after some research, we found no reference to her existence, not even an obituary.

"We would find that in Manitowoc," I replied.

"I guess I wasn't very important to the greater world," she concluded.

"Now, now," I said. "You influenced some very important Wagner children who later became successful, not to mention famous! You were a maid, not a child nor an ancestor in the main family, so sometimes important people like you are lost to history."

"I am tired of always being dismissed as just a maid!" Elsa continued. "I was a member of the family, a real person, a parent, a child of God, just like anyone else!"

"You are correct," I conceded.

"Elsa, when I started researching Alfred, I had only his gravestone, the church entry for his death, and some oral history. By the time I finished, I had two deeds, a marriage certificate, two news articles and several additional stories from distant relatives. Information is often somewhere out of sight just waiting to be found.

"However, I know of much information on Alfred that was also gone," I continued. "All the records of Alfred's service as Justice of The Peace were lost when the town office burned with the general store in Cleveland in 1930. I couldn't find any naturalization record for him in Wisconsin or in New York State where he stayed for his first six months in America. The passport Alfred showed me in 1858 did not survive. No letters were found."

"Christina would have burned them," Elsa said.

"You know that Alfred died before I did," Elsa continued.

"Yes, I knew that. What happened?" I asked.

"We didn't know for sure, but the doctor thought it was a gall bladder problem," Elsa said.

"I had that. It was fixed with surgery," I replied.

"Christina was devastated when Alfred died," Elsa continued. "Young Ludwig had to grow up in a hurry."

"He did well for himself, thanks in part to your tutoring."

"I found several other Alfred Wagners in various national records while I was doing my research," I added. "But none matched his data. And I was unable to find anything on Alfred when I went to Detmold. I did find another Wagner there named Herman, a glassmaker, a few years younger than Alfred. Herman's father was named Johann. I was thinking that Herman may have been a brother to Alfred."

Elsa could not recall the names of Alfred's parents or siblings but said that the name Herman sounded familiar. She thought that he was the one corresponding with Alfred over the years.

"We will go there!" Elsa suddenly shouted. "We will go to Germany!"

"Absolutely!" I shouted back. "You can find your way through the files, the old German stuff, much better than I could! Yes! Yes!"

Chapter 60 – Cemetery

We spent the remainder of the day on the Saxon Cemetery. We visited the graves of Alfred, Junior, Christina, Ludwig, and Natalie. Heinrich Wagner was buried in Milwaukee, Otto in Shawano. Emma and Tina were buried on other local cemeteries.

There were several other graves of Wagner descendants who were born after Elsa's time. She asked many questions about them. Sometimes she would say, "That's a typical Wagner, that's what Alfred and Christina would have done!"

Elsa recounted the people whom she did know that were buried there, more than a hundred in number. I knew several of them from my previous mission, but not in such detail. The tour of the cemetery took a couple of hours. We agreed to come back another day. I told her that what she said needed to be recorded.

Just when we were leaving the cemetery, Elsa said, "My brother Arlen is buried over there." She pointed to a spot near the utility building. We walked over to the stone, set flat in the ground and almost covered with the lawn. Elsa aggressively dug the grass away with her hands to expose the entire stone as if it were suddenly urgent to retain its memory. The stone was now hard to read.

"What a shame!" she muttered. "Can we put a new stone here too?"

"Absolutely!"

I didn't say anything about Arlen, knowing how much Arlen's death hurt Elsa. Not in the past nor in the present would Elsa ever tell Arlen's story.

There were two old stones next to Arlen's, also suicides. Those stones were also laid flat and now impossible to read. The early suicides were shunned, their bodies buried distant from other graves with flat stones. Later those who took their own lives were buried with their respective families.

Killing oneself was considered the equivalent of murder in past times, an act likely to land one in hell. Later suicides were recognized more sympathetically as unfortunate acts of troubled people.

CHAPTER 61 – EDNA

After Centerville, Elsa spent a few weeks with me in Madison. We drove over to Milwaukee to see her granddaughter Edna, a woman in her nineties, much older now, of course, than Elsa herself. Elsa disguised her real identity as I requested, but it was hard to keep Elsa from saying too much. After all, we were talking to her granddaughter, her closest kin and someone she may have known had she lived a normal lifespan. It appeared that Elsa wanted to hug her granddaughter and could barely restrain herself

Edna recalled memories of her mother and stories of Elsa. Not all of what was said about Elsa was correct. Edna complained about the man she had heard that left Elsa in 1870 and broke her heart. At this point, I was even tempted to correct the narrative and expose Elsa, however we kept our secrets to ourselves, just asking more questions. Elsa was happy to get more details on story of her daughter Anita, Edna's mother.

We asked Edna if we could make copies of the photographs of the Anita and other members of her family. There was one of Elsa herself. Edna commented on how much my friend Elsa resembled the old photograph of Elsa. Elsa almost couldn't contain her emotions after that comment. Elsa would later cuddle with those photos for hours.

"Imagine if we had told Edna the truth," I told Elsa later. "She would not have believed us, of course. She would likely have gotten angry and told us to leave. Or worse, she would have had a mental crisis or a heart attack!"

"We need to visit her again soon!" Elsa stated forcefully. "Regardless of what you said, she must know who I am!"

I told Elsa to restrain herself. "Think about how difficult it would be to tell her the truth," I emphasized. The potential confrontation would never happen. We didn't know it at the time, but we would never see Edna again.

CHAPTER 62 – STAYING

Elsa confirmed her desire to stay in the present. She wasn't having as much of a hard time dealing with complexity of the present as she was in dealing with her memories. However, the more she considered, the more she longed to stay.

"This is such an incredible adventure!" she said. "We are so fortunate to have this time travel and live two lives!" Elsa said for about the 20th time. "I have nothing to go back to. I have died once," she said. "So, the second time, if that's what happens, will not be as difficult. Knowing that there is the possibility of a second life makes living so much more worthwhile. I also want to tell the world the truth about our missions and bring other people back from the past."

"In due time," I countered.

Elsa and I spent considerable time discussing what we knew and didn't know about our supernatural experience. All we knew was that we were contacted subconsciously about our missions and that they did indeed happen. My desire to bring Elsa to my present was honored and communicated to me before I left in 1870. God, someone, something beyond our comprehension considered us to be special, a valued experiment, a fulfillment of destiny, a wonderful love story to be continued. The physics of time travel, the retention of our spiritual information and the possibility of re-incarnation did indeed exist.

We still hadn't found the afterlife of paradise promised by religion. Elsa had experienced a kind of limbo, one could say, between her two lives. If she had indeed spent time in another universe, she couldn't remember it. Neither could I remember anything about my transitions between past and present. My disappearance from the present for twelve years was a kind of time warp that probably took no more than a few moments of a dream.

I took Elsa in as a domestic partner, put her on my insurance, and began teaching her to drive a car.

It was a difficult process to get Elsa a proper identity, however. We developed a convoluted story that Elsa was born on the run in Eastern Europe at the end World War II, abandoned in a German orphanage, raised by a foster family for a while, and that her birth was unregistered and exact birthdate unknown. She entered the United States without documentation. We felt like we had never lied so much in our lives, although up to 1870, I was surely something of an expert on lying!

In the end, there was no place to send her back to, so she got a delayed refugee status. I told the immigration authorities that we were engaged to be married and I would therefore be supporting her.

Although Elsa and I were doing and saying everything we needed to as if moving quickly toward marriage, Elsa was surprised by my sudden and previously unannounced marriage proposal in front of the immigration authorities. She was nonetheless thrilled by my commitment.

After we were outside of the immigration office, Elsa shouted, "There you said it! I wanted you to say it for 12 years while we were together in the past and you never did! I now understand why. I'm sorry I was so hard on you sometimes. But really, I didn't understand!"

"I know," I replied. "I'm sorry about all of that too. I had a hard time explaining myself, especially with all your questions and doubts. You were not part of the plan then. You certainly are now!"

"Are you going to get on one knee for me to make it formal, a bit more romantic?" Elsa asked.

"If you need," I replied, getting on my knee.

Chapter 63 – Wedding

Elsa and I got married on the Wagner farm in the cow yard on top of the cobblestones where the housebarn had once stood. My nephew David thought it was a strange idea but went through great effort to clear off the manure and dirt from the stones. There were some comments about how unromantic it was to get married in a cow yard.

It was a small wedding attended by two dozen people, insignificant to the world, but of monumental importance to a family and to science. No one else at the wedding had any idea of who Elsa really was or how far we had traveled to get there!

David and a University friend of mine named Karen served as our witnesses. For our wedding music, we chose the Radetsky March by Johann Strauss, Sr. and New Horizons by the Moody Blues.

David was keeping heifers for the neighboring farmer. He locked them out of the cow yard for the wedding. When I realized that they were Jerseys, I asked David to let them back in after the ceremony. The Wagner farm had owned a herd of Jerseys for 90 years. I grew up with the breed.

We were still standing in the cow yard when the Jerseys came back in. They are curious, friendly cattle. They came right up to greet me, trying to lick my hand and chew my clothes. It was as if they knew that I was a "Jersey guy." In fact, I had a Jersey tattoo on my arm. I gently patted them on their heads. Even though I was no longer farming, I was always happy to have another Jersey moment now and then.

Elsa was not so impressed about having cows crash our wedding. But I said, "Let them, they also have right to be here. Jerseys have a long history on these cobblestones, longer than the housebarn ever did!" I reminded Elsa of Alfred's favorite cow.

Fortunately, I was not wearing anything that was entirely made of cotton. Had I been, the cows would have been happy to rip it off me. Cotton, which is cellulose, is totally digestible to ruminants!

My daughters Sarah and Jennifer attended the wedding, of course. Sarah, a teacher, was raising her family. Jennifer, still single, was employed by the University. Both were quite surprised about Elsa and our quick marriage. As much as I wanted to spill our incredible secrets at the wedding, all I could say was that I would explain it all sometime later.

Elsa and I walked out to the woods as we had done many times before, but this time we stripped and walked naked for about a half hour. We didn't care if anyone was watching!

The modest wedding reception that evening was held at the dance hall where Elsa and I had danced for the last time over a century before. It was the last of four dance halls that had once existed in Cleveland and Centerville. Two had burned and one was purchased and moved to the county historical village. We hired an orchestra that could play our song, the Elsa Polka. Before we walked out, we announced that our honeymoon would be in Germany, visiting both the former Lippe-Detmold and Saxony.

While we were in Germany, that dance hall also burned down. The report stated that the fire accidently started in the kitchen when no one was around. Everyone in the community believed it was an intentional insurance fire started by the owner who was losing money. Our dance was the building's last event, the Elsa Polka the last song. The last venue of polka music in the Centerville area was now gone.

Elsa and I spent eight weeks in Germany. We found only a few distant relatives. There were some records on the Wagners, my side of the family in Detmold. There was nothing about Alfred's duel. Police records from the time had long been discarded. We could find no newspaper accounts. The Wagner glassmakers were long gone. After two World Wars, many Germans were uprooted to other locations. Since I was not born in Germany, I had no memories there.

Elsa easily located her home village in Saxony. The house she was born in no longer existed. There were no Jacobys left. The graves of her Jacoby family members in Saxony no longer existed. Europeans commonly recycle graves after a certain number of years.

However, records of Meyers and other relatives were found in city archives and church-record offices. We revisited the church records for Christina, some of which had been centralized in Meissen, the county seat.

Edna passed away while we were in Europe. She would never know our secret.

Elsa and I traveled to Czech Republic and Austria at the end of our trip. We attended a Strauss concert in Vienna. After the concert, we strolled through a park in Vienna where we found a stump of a recently cut tree to sit on. It was a new beginning.

Elsa and I waited a year before sharing our time travel secrets with my daughters, nieces, nephews and other relatives in Wisconsin. We decided to first write a book about it.

EPILOGUE

Centerville is a personal venture into my past, based in Town Centerville in Manitowoc County, Wisconsin where I grew up. The book adds a powerful but fictitious love story. Much of the book centers around the Wiegand farm, my home farm, established in 1848, and the immediate neighborhood. The farm, called the Wagner farm in the book, is still owned by the family as I write today. Although I have considerable knowledge of the history of the farm and the neighborhood, I had to use my imagination for many of the details in the narrative.

Most of the events and persons portrayed were either real or had some basis in reality. The names of people have been changed and events obscured to provide confidentiality, although some locals will probably know who and what I am talking about. The names of local businesses have been changed or omitted. Events have been altered to fit the narrative and the time period. No harm is intended anywhere in the book. Real place names are used, however. Those who want to know the exact history should contact me or other local sources.

Part One of the book details my mission, as I call it, for me to travel from the present back in time to visit my ancestors in 1858. I planned to only stay for a few months. The mission becomes complicated and extended to a dozen years by the fact that I fall in love with Elsa, the Wagner maid.

Elsa is totally fictional, although I designated her as a relative of the original male settler on the Wiegand farm. I named her after the Elsa Polka, also known as the Elsie Polka, my favorite Romy Gosz Orchestra polka that I often heard when I was growing up. Romy Gosz, a Bohemian-American and first-class trumpet player who got the attention of the big bands, was considered the Polka King in Eastern Wisconsin from the 1930s-60s. I saw him and his orchestra many times.

I created Elsa's character as a frontier woman with a more modern, liberated attitude. My image of Elsa is partially based on a brief story of a first-generation Wiegand daughter who died in 1890 during childbirth at age thirty-seven. Elsa's image is also a reflection of the character and personality of a forty-year friend of mine.

My hope is that this book will someday be made into a movie. A percentage of the net proceeds from the book and movie are to be used as a fundraiser for a library for Centreville Settlement Inc, a historical preservation organization in Town Centerville that I helped to establish in 1982. The library, mentioned near the end of the book, does not yet exist but is a dream of mine.

I would hope that Romy Gosz music, with his version of the Elsa Polka, would be featured in any future movie and be the closing music for the movie. I would further hope that the movie will feature Town Centerville actors in some the of the minor roles. Should I still be around, I would also want a brief appearance in the movie.

My writings are always intended to be informative and education-al, hence the extensive historical descriptions. Much of it relates to my background in agriculture. There is considerable commentary from my modern perspective. Even when I don't provide commentary, my personal life and perspective are hinted at in the book. I hope that you, the reader, will be both entertained and informed.

It was my intention to honor the contributions of my German ancestors and their neighbors, and to illustrate their struggles settling in the New World. As always, we must remember that what we have today was built upon the sacrifices and foundations established by those who came before us.

One challenge in writing this book was to generate enough words for a typical novel. It's not that I don't have enough to say. My background in writing is scientific and educational where one does not waste words on description but gets to the point. Modern readers tend to have shorter attention span, so longer may not be better. Another challenge for me was to add fiction to history, a clear violation of my historical side. I forced myself to do this, however, in pursuit of a rich story and to fill gaps in the history.

I wrote the book in modern American English for simplicity's sake. It would have been too time-consuming to research and adopt all the usage and expressions of the mid-1800s. I did try to eliminate some of the modern jargon that Elsa and others speaking English would not have known. The historical assumption is that German was spoken most of the time in conversation in Part One and English in Part Two. Realistically, the movie would be made in English with occasional German expressions.

I have been asked by a local historian to divulge the true names of three important "destinations" referred by other names in the book. The New Settlement Tavern is the Hika Bay Tavern, the Leitner Housebarn is the Lutze Housebarn, and the Leipzig House in Fredonia, Wisconsin is the Saxonia House established by the Klessig families.

Although I talk about time travel in the book, mentioning specific missions, I did not describe how I was able to travel back in time, or how Elsa was able to visit me in the present. This was not intended to be a science fiction book. You, the reader, are left to imagine how this would work.

I would like to thank the following persons who proofread the book for me—Sherrie Wiegand, my wife, and a retired psychiatric social worker; Alan Pape, an author, local historian, historic building expert, and co-founder of Old-World Wisconsin historical museum; Janet Lutze, my third cousin, a retired medical professional, former Centerville resident (Lutze Housebarn), and co-founder and long-time President of Centreville Settlement, Inc; Sarah Schnuelle, my niece, a teacher, and reading and writing specialist, with her husband Craig; Jennifer Blazek, a close friend, former University of Wisconsin Extension colleague, and Director of University of Wisconsin Farm & Industry Short Course program; Fern Kanitz, a close friend, family mediation specialist, former University of Wisconsin graduate school colleague, and former Peace Corps volunteer like myself, with her husband Arthur; Gerry and Elise Klessig Heimerl, former farm neighbors, and retired Centerville farmers and cheesemakers; and David Jacoby, a business entrepreneur and environmentalist, with his wife Shari.

I would further like to thank the several coffee houses where much of my book was written, including The Dock and Alley Cats Coffee, both in Spooner, Wisconsin, and Mother Fools and Einstein Coffee & Bagels in Madison, Wisconsin.

THE AUTHOR

Richard Otto Wiegand was born on September 20, 1948 and grew up on the Wiegand Farm in Town Centerville in Manitowoc County, Wisconsin. The Wiegand farm has been in the family since 1848. Richard operated the farm in the 1980s. Local and family history were common topics at the dinner table. Richard started doing family research in his 30s and has never stopped. That research included two trips to Germany (1987, 2003).

Richard attained three Degrees in Dairy Science (BS, MS, PhD) from the University of Wisconsin-Madison, in addition to an MA in African Studies from Ohio University. He was employed by University of Wisconsin Cooperative Extension in Northwest Wisconsin from 2004 until he retired in 2017.

Richard has done considerable international work, serving in the US Peace Crops in Kenya and Paraguay, conducting graduate research in Ethiopia and consulting with the African Development Bank in Ivory Coast. He has done Farmer-to-Farmer and other short-term projects in more than a dozen other countries. Richard received an Honorary

Recognition Award for his international work from the University of Wisconsin, College of Agriculture and Life Sciences, in 2016.

Richard was a co-founder of Centreville Settlement, Inc. in 1982, a Centerville historic preservation group and served as Vice-President, President and Board Member. He was also a co-founder of The Greater Centerville Historians that collected Centerville oral history from 2000-2015. Richard is the author of *Silos of Manitowoc County* (1989), a best-selling monograph for the Manitowoc County Historical Society. He has been a member the Manitowoc County Historical Society, the Sheboygan County Society and Sheboygan County Historical Research Center for over thirty years.

Richard has written numerous articles, presentations and reports. He is currently writing his family history, his autobiography, and has at least two other books in progress.

www.ingramcontent.com/pod-product-compliance
Lightning Source LLC
Chambersburg PA
CBHW071356100726
47908CB00004B/1012